She was a pawn in an outlandish scheme

Diana led an idyllic life. Rich and beautiful, she could afford to indulge any whim . . . until she learned the truth that sent her world crashing.

For years the family business had been suffering financial difficulty. Now it teetered on the brink of disaster. Its main investor, Andrew Chamberland, offered an outrageous choice: the company could go bankrupt . . . or Diana could marry him.

Diana was desperately confused. How could she possibly marry a man she didn't love? But if she didn't, she would drag her family into ruin.

Fatal Choice

by JEAN D'ASTOR

MYSTIQUE BOOKS

TORONTO • LONDON • NEW YORK
HAMBURG • AMSTERDAM • STOCKHOLM

FATAL CHOICE / first published October 1980

All the characters in this book have no existence outside the
imagination of the author and have no relation whatsoever to
anyone bearing the same name or names. They are not even
distantly inspired by any individual known or unknown to the
author, and all the incidents are pure invention.

The Mystique Books trademark, consisting of the words MYSTIQUE
BOOKS and the logotype, is registered in the Canada Trade Marks
Office, the United States Patent Office, and in other countries.

ISBN 0-373-50098-X

PRINTED IN U.S.A.

Chapter 1

"Whoa, Prince!"

The lithe girl dressed casually in a white shirt, faded blue jeans and sandals, pulled back hard on the reins. The radiant smile that had lighted her features only moments before slowly disappeared.

Diana's brows drew together and her face hardened as Prince came to a stop in the middle of the clearing known as Templars' Crossing.

"Look," she muttered, "just look at what they've done to this beautiful forest!"

Freshly cut logs were piled on either side of the path. Beyond, where tall trees had once stood, there was only a wide expanse of land that had been stripped almost bare. The harsh June sunlight revealed a few remaining trees that had been granted a temporary reprieve only because the loggers hadn't had time to fell them.

"What a sight!"

With clenched teeth Diana fought back tears brought on by the sight of the beeches and oaks lying among the ferns.

Even the avenue itself had been despoiled; bulldozers had bitten savagely into its surface, leaving deep tracks in their wake. All that remained of the bushes that flowered pink and gold in spring and were laden with mulberries in summer were a few dead branches and dry leaves.

"Let's go, Prince. I don't want to come back this way ever again!"

As she rode off, Diana felt she was leaving part of her childhood behind. Her heart was heavy with memories—memories that had virtually been destroyed along with the desecration of the forest. She could feel her anger rising, directed not against the loggers who were pillaging her forest or the man who paid them to do so—for he was well within his rights—but against her stepfather. For some time now he had been doing precious little except sell off the estate, piece by piece.

And yet there was no apparent cause for such a sacrifice. The textile mill was running smoothly, the value of the cattle had not diminished one iota, and the stud horses fetched prices that Diana herself deemed exorbitant.

She could not fathom the reason for her stepfather's financial problems. Month by month they grew more serious, driving Proust to desperate measures that suggested he was on the verge of bankruptcy.

Diana rode on in pensive silence for several

minutes and then, little by little, regained her feeling of serenity.

After a few minutes she arrived at a spot where the trees stood out against a vast backdrop of blue and gold—Shady Oak Pond, named after the original mansion built on the estate. Ducks and herons flocked to its banks, and by night poachers crept stealthily into the estate to fish in it. Diana rode toward the water over a pathway that was a carpet of sand and thick grass.

From the time she had been allowed to wander about by herself, Diana had spent more time at the pond than in her own bedroom. She wondered now how long it would be before this tranquil spot would also be destroyed.

She drew closer to the pond, whose glistening surface made her blink after the cool shadows of the forest. On the right, a few stone steps covered with moss led into the blue green depths of the pool. Diana dismounted and knelt motionless at the water's edge for several seconds, suspended between two skies, smiling at her reflection and savoring the refreshing breeze that caressed her face.

Then she saw him.

The shock almost sent her tumbling into the water. A cry died on her lips as she stood, her eyes wide. She was absolutely dumbfounded at the extraordinary apparition that had suddenly emerged from the depths of the pond. It was a man. His torso was bare, the wet muscles glistening in the sunlight. He stared at her boldly.

"Hello." His voice was deep, calm. "Where did *you* spring from?"

Diana regained her composure quickly and assumed an air of cold hauteur. "Never mind that. Just what do you think *you're* doing here?" she demanded.

The intruder frowned, as if pondering the question.

"Now, let me think. . . . Cold water always has disastrous effects on my memory. I know that I got into this pond for an express purpose, but the exact nature of it . . . ."

"Didn't you see the signs?"

"Of course I did. That's precisely what gave me the idea to come here. I decided this place must be special, simply because there were so many precautions taken to keep people out. First I took a road with a white gate and a sign marked Private Property, then a little later I came across a path and a No Trespassing sign. Finally I came to the pond where I noticed the No Fishing or Swimming Allowed sign. Then I got into the water."

Diana was at a loss for words. How dared this insolent stranger make fun of her! She was almost choking on her indignation, but the intruder appeared not to notice and concluded calmly, "And I was right. This place is charming, and the owner has every reason to keep people out. I couldn't bear to see a bunch of Sunday picnickers ruining such a romantic setting!"

But you are ruining it now for me, Diana thought angrily. *This has always been my spot—my secret refuge from the rest of the world.* She fixed the intruder with a cold stare and was nonplussed to see a smile twitching his lips.

"You are quite correct about one thing," she began with an impressive coolness she did not feel. "Since the owners of these woods do not tolerate vagrants, they're prepared to go to any lengths to keep them out. I'm in a position to say so, since the owners happen to be my parents."

The stranger advanced a few inches, his jaws hardening almost imperceptibly. Before he had the chance to open his mouth Diana continued, "I must inform you that by disregarding the signs, you could very easily be prosecuted."

The stranger was still for a moment, but his eyes glinted dangerously, then he smiled. "That's enough of the law; now what about humanity? While you stand there playing lady of the manor, I'm catching a cold. This water is freezing!"

Stung by his words, Diana flew off the handle. "Well, why don't you get out? You shouldn't be here in the first place!"

The young man smiled, a slow, lazy relaxing of his lips that made him suddenly seem attractive. He started wading toward her, his curiously light eyes locked on hers. "All right, though I feel I should warn you, I haven't a stitch of clothing on."

"Y-you're joking," she stammered.

"Am I?" He still advanced toward her, the level of the water now almost to his waist.

"Wait!" Diana cried.

The young man stopped, an eyebrow raised quizzically "Well?" he drawled.

Diana decided that she couldn't stay there any

longer without making an embarrassing situation worse. She jumped onto Prince and impatiently dug her heels into him. "Come on, Prince. Let's go."

Then throwing a cutting glance at the intruder, she rode off into the trees, her cheeks flaming at the mocking laugh that followed her.

Chapter 2

The day was definitely not going well. As Diana rode along she glanced over the wall surrounding the stables and grimaced. Beyond the lawns, parked at the front steps of the house, was a flashy American car. There was no mistaking it, even at such a distance. It was flaming red and chrome-laden, and somehow called to her mind a large slab of rare roast beef.

The young woman stopped her horse. "About face, Prince! Emilie will no doubt be glad to see us. Let's go to Hazel Farm."

Hazel Farm was a ranch with lush pastures that were the home of some hundred Norman cattle. It was part of the large estate that had been in Diana's family for generations. Diana, her mother and stepfather lived in Shady Oaks, a graceful mansion that had been built by Louis Cavalier, Diana's great-great-grandfather. Louis's full-length portrait still occupied a place of honor in the drawing room and his name was always mentioned in tones of grateful respect. It was he who was responsible for the bulk of the family's present wealth.

Prince retraced his steps until he reached the path leading to the forest. He passed the walls of the abandoned orange groves, and turned of his own accord onto a tree-shaded path. At the end of the path was an exquisite Norman cottage topped by a thatched roof and surrounded by a profusion of flowers. As they emerged from the canopy of trees, a series of freshly painted farm buildings came into view, bathed in the pink rays of the late-afternoon sun.

"Miss Diana! You're just in time to sample my jam!"

Upon hearing the clip-clop of the horse's hooves, a woman had appeared on the doorstep, wiping her hands on her blue apron. She was in her thirties, had a generous figure, a rosy complexion and an ingenuous smile. Diana dismounted and kissed her on both cheeks.

"Is that what smells so good? I could smell it all the way up the path."

Emilie laughed. "I've been cooking all afternoon! Look!" She pulled Diana inside the cottage.

Almost one hundred jars were lined up on the newspaper-covered oak table. An acid-sweet aroma floated in the large room with its beamed ceiling.

"The only problem is that I had the stove going for hours, and now it's like an oven in here. Would you like a piece of bread and jam?"

Diana smiled in reply. She remembered the days

when Emilie worked for her parents. At the time Emilie couldn't have been more than eighteen or nineteen, and was unable to turn down any request from Diana. She stuffed the child with goodies at all hours of the day. The result was that at mealtime her little charge rarely ate a mouthful, to Diana's parents' deep chagrin.

Today Emilie and her husband managed Hazel Farm, one of the most successful farms in the area. They had two sons, six and eight, whom she shooed out of the house to play whenever they asked for between-meal treats.

"Aren't Jason and Timmy home from school yet?"

"They won't be back until six tonight, thank goodness! It's so much easier to work without those little rascals underfoot!"

Diana sat down at the end of the table and bit into her bread enthusiastically. Emilie uncorked a bottle of cider and filled two glasses.

"So you managed to escape," Emilie said slowly.

Her choice of words surprised Diana, who raised her eyebrows in amusement. Emilie seemed embarrassed, as if she had committed some gaffe.

"I mean . . . I thought . . . since your parents have a guest . . . ."

Diana burst out laughing.

"I can see you're right up-to-date on what's happening at the house!"

"Fernand, the new game warden, came by more than an hour ago. He mentioned that Mr. Chamberland had arrived. I take it you weren't at home when he arrived?"

"I went for a ride right after lunch. . . ." Diana paused, as the image of a tall bronzed man flashed through her mind. For a moment she was disconcerted by the sudden wrenching feeling in the pit of her stomach that the image induced.

Emilie's voice prodded her back to the subject at hand. "And . . .?"

Diana firmly pushed the image from her mind. "On my way back I noticed the car, and decided to take refuge here."

At Emilie's expression Diana hastened to explain.

"I didn't want to run into him dressed like this. Mr. Chamberland always looks so smart!"

"A little too smart for the country, wouldn't you say?"

"True. He always looks as if he's on his way to the theater."

Emilie lapsed into silence and then ventured hesitantly, "Probably because he hopes to make a good impression on someone. . . ."

"Probably." Diana shrugged. "It's quite obvious that Chamberland is courting me. But I'm not exactly proud of it. I'd just as soon avoid him!"

"But it's flattering, all the same! He's not bad looking, and he's got lots of money. Lots of women must be after him."

"Could be. But I don't love him, and I have no intention of getting married to him. I want only one thing from him: that he stop destroying my forest!"

Diana's eyes misted over as she stared at an immense clearing strewn with dead trees beyond the farm buildings. Then she corrected herself.

"I mean, what *used* to be our forest. You wouldn't recognize Templars' Crossing. There isn't even a crossroad left—nothing but empty land. What I can't understand is why my parents even sold him the land. For the past few months they've been selling off property like mad! First The Circle R, which was one of our most successful operations—"

"True, but the roof needed replacing and the piggery was falling apart."

"Then the meadows over toward Chambray. And now the Cavalier Forests. At this rate, soon they'll be selling Shady Oaks and Hazel Farm. Oh, Emilie! You and I could be out of our homes!"

Emilie was dismayed to see how Diana's voice trembled and her eyes glistened with tears. She put her arm around the young woman's shoulders and said soothingly, "There, there. Now, don't get all upset. I daresay if the day came when I had to leave my home, I'd manage. And so would you. I understand how you feel about seeing the land pass into someone else's hands, but don't go overdramatizing things. There are lots of people who will never own a tenth of what you still have left."

Emilie's matter-of-fact reasoning had the desired effect.

Diana felt her self-pity dissolve. "You're right, of course. I must sound like a spoiled brat. But it's not really the . . . the value of the land I was thinking about. It's just that everything seems to be changing around me—everything that has been a part of my life for so long." Diana sighed. "I'm not making much sense, am I?"

Emilie smiled. "Lots of sense, my dear. You're just finding out how painful growing up is sometimes. You're barely out of your teens, and you've been sheltered all your life, surrounded by constancy and love." Emilie sighed. "Be thankful for that, at least."

Diana squeezed Emilie's hand. "You're a true friend, Emilie. And I am thankful for the life I've had. But you see, the forest reminds me of papa."

Again Diana gazed into the distance, her eyes filled with sadness and longing. "When father learned that he was about to die, he would take mother and me there every day. I can still see him in his leather boots and gray felt hat, and now I realize how young he was. . . ."

Emilie nodded. "Yes, it was a terrible time for all of us."

"He was the same age as Andrew Chamberland—not quite forty," Diana said. "And as Chamberland's the one who walks through the forest, deciding which trees to destroy . . . . Oh, I don't hold it against him personally; he's a businessman. He can't let himself be influenced by sentiment."

"Who knows? Perhaps if you asked him . . .?"

Diana shook her head decisively. "Don't you see, he's not at the root of the trouble— it's my stepfather who is selling the land. I just can't understand what's driving him to do it!"

"Probably he needs the money," Emilie said dryly.

"But why? It's been going on for a year now, even though nothing has changed. The factory is making a profit, the farms are making a profit, even the horses—"

"That remains to be seen," Emilie interrupted. "As far as the horses are concerned, Mark, the head groom, was telling me just last night how expensive that operation is. When you take everything into account—fodder, vet bills, staff, upkeep on the stables, the taxes that the state deducts from every purse we win, not to mention how much it costs when a prize horse has an accident and has to be slaughtered like a cow—"

"I know, but not too long ago—"

"And who told you that your parents aren't down to their last penny trying to keep up with it all? The big estates are on the way out. Upkeep is more and more expensive, and the taxes just get higher and higher." Emilie was in full flight.

Despite herself, Diana had to laugh.

"If you're trying to reassure me, you're having just the opposite effect!"

Emilie regained her composure and said less heatedly, "I'm just trying to help you look at things realistically. To accept the inevitable is one way to avoid unnecessary suffering."

At that moment, a man perched on an old bicycle rode into the courtyard. Diana recognized the game warden, who also doubled as gatekeeper to Shady Oaks.

"Here's Fernand, back from his rounds in the forest," Emilie idly remarked. Then she glanced at the clock and said, "That's strange. He's usually back much earlier than this."

Once more a sudden image of a mocking smile and flashing eyes seared Diana's thoughts. Perhaps Fernand had run into the mysterious swimmer. That would explain his late return. It would serve the man right if Fernand slapped a heavy fine on him. A small smile played on the corners of Diana's lips.

Noticing the sudden change of mood, Emilie's eyebrows lifted in inquiry.

Diana couldn't resist trying to explain. "I met someone strange in the forest when I was riding. Perhaps Fernand ran across him, too. Maybe that's why he's so late getting back from his rounds."

Emilie grew anxious. "You met someone today?"

"Just now. In the pond."

"What do you mean, *in* the pond?"

"He was swimming. Anyway, I assume he was, since he was up to his neck in water."

"That must have been a relief. At least it gave you time to get away. You'd better be more careful in the future. You never know who's hiding out in the forests."

"This one didn't look dangerous to me. He was rather cheeky, though."

"What was he like? Young? Old?"

"Young. About thirty."

"Well dressed?"

Diana laughed. "Hardly. He made a point of telling me that he was completely nude."

"Oh!" Emilie blushed.

"Don't worry. And don't look so scandalized! He didn't come out of the water." No need to mention the man's threat to do so. "Anyway, I saw his clothes on the bank and they looked quite acceptable to me: jeans and a sport shirt."

"Was he good-looking?"

"I think so. . . . Actually, I was so furious that I didn't really pay much attention."

"Why?"

"Because he was swimming in my pond, that's why! And because I caught him red-handed and it didn't worry him in the least!"

"Was he some sort of vagrant?" Emilie probed.

"I don't know. They come in all shapes and sizes, you know."

"It was probably someone on vacation—one of the villager's relatives. Maybe Miss Remy's nephew; she owns the dry-goods store. But he doesn't strike me as the type who would go in for swimming. He's a tall blond, a little on the thin side. . . ."

Diana frowned slightly in concentration. "This one had brown hair and looked rather athletic."

"Then I have no idea who it could be."

"Oh, let's forget it. It's not important." Diana glanced at the clock. "I suppose I should be getting back. The coast is probably clear by now. Our dear friend probably got tired of waiting for me and gave up."

As she rose she added, "I'd like to know what it is he's after that he still hasn't got from us. I don't know why, but he gives me the creeps."

"Well, I still think you ought to give him a chance. But if he does want anything—besides you, that is—you'll soon find out from your parents."

"I doubt it. For the last little while everything has been one big secret. My stepfather has been unusually edgy. I've asked my mother about it, but she just shrugs and tells me she knows nothing about what's going on. After all, my stepfather manages all our affairs."

"Just the same, your mother must have had to sign *something* in order for your stepfather to sell the properties you mentioned!" Emilie remarked.

"Naturally. And she must have had good reason to agree to such drastic measures."

"Haven't you ever discussed it with her?"

"I've tried several times. But she's always made it clear that she thinks I'm too young to have a hand in such matters," Diana said.

"What about Mrs. Faber?"

"Grandmother? You know what she's like—the soul of discretion. I don't know whether she ever takes the liberty of giving her own daughter advice. And she's even more reserved with her second son-in-law. Of course, she's never really cared for him."

"There's nothing surprising about that. She loved your father as if he were her son," Emilie said.

"I know. It's all so confused and complicated. I wish I were older. Perhaps I'd be able to see things differently. But in the meantime I can't help wondering whether my stepfather . . . ."

Diana made a vague gesture and fell silent. She had discovered herself thinking aloud. "You're probably bored to death by all this. I'm sorry!"

"You know that you—"

"I know—I can count on your friendship and support. If you hear any rumors about the business . . . ."

"Rest assured; you'll be the first to know."

But Diana failed to notice that as Emilie made her promise she lowered her gaze and her cheeks colored even mo.e.

CHAMBERLAND WAS MORE than a little put out that Diana had not been at Shady Oaks to greet him. She seldom seemed to be around when he called. For a fleeting moment he wondered if she was avoiding him, but almost at once decided that that was ridiculous. He had been very circumspect in his dealings with her; there was no reason why she should avoid him.

He shrugged. No matter. What he had to discuss with her stepfather would improve the situation considerably.

Now he preceded Jack Proust into the study. As usual, as soon as the two men were alone their faces changed completely. It was as if each stripped off a mask.

In front of others, they played the role of two old friends who were delighted to see each other. Both were so cordial, polite and jovial that everyone marveled at their friendship. But the minute the door closed behind them, the facade melted away. Proust's face took on an expression of mistrust, fear, and at times even hatred. As for Chamberland, although he continued to smile, his face reflected nothing more than arrogant contempt.

That day their meeting began in silence. Proust sat down at his desk while Chamberland remained standing. He opened a briefcase, took out a file and flipped through it before tossing it on the desk.

"The new orders," he said in a neutral tone of voice. "Enough to keep the mill going for another two months."

It was difficult to tell Chamberland's age by looking at him. He could be anywhere between thirty and forty. He had a narrow face, pale skin, and thin lips. His manner was cold, and he gave the impression of weighing every word he uttered. He never answered any question right away, even the most innocuous one. He seemed to be looking for some hidden meaning behind the words.

Proust scanned the papers. Without looking up he murmured, "This is a small order. There was no need to make a trip to Paris for this!"

The other man laughed softly.

"It sounds as if you don't quite know me. The trip was necessary. I had things to arrange. Rest assured, there will be other trips, more expensive than this one. But I won't be going anywhere for a while yet. I'd like to see how our . . . little project turns out. Understand?"

Proust stared at him in silence. Chamberland casually went on with his explanation. "It would be stupid of me to give your mill all my business if it's only going to close down. Not only would it complicate liquidation, my buyers would have to wait for delivery of their merchandise. So it pays me to keep on good terms with my other suppliers in Paris. And I have quite a number of those!"

"I know! In other words, this is a new twist to your blackmail! If you get what you want, the Cavalier Mill will get the money it needs. Otherwise—"

"Otherwise it will be the end of the company. And out of charity I'll give it a little helping hand so that its death throes won't last too long."

He dropped into an armchair with a sigh. "But what's the use of going over that again? You've known all along the logic of my viewpoint."

"Logic! The logic of crooks and swindlers!"

Chamberland didn't flinch at the insult. He took a small leather case out of his pocket and began to clean his nails.

"You always use such nasty words! And you always force me to remind you of certain things that took place in the past. But perhaps you're right this time. We should forget the past, since the deciding hand is about to be dealt. Don't you think we should both take a look at our cards?"

Chapter 3

The red car had disappeared. Yet, instead of crossing the lawn, Diana made a detour through the kitchen garden. That way she could go in the back door and straight up to her bedroom by taking a small staircase located between the kitchen and the laundry room.

Whenever she came back from a ride in the forest she felt vaguely guilty and tried to avoid running into her mother. Mrs. Proust was quite unable to fathom how a pretty young woman of twenty could enjoy herself for hours on end in the forest, with only trees, sun and wind for company.

In the eyes of her ever elegant mother—for whom life took on significance only at a party or in a casino—love of solitude was not only morbid, but indicative of some sort of mental imbalance. Equally incomprehensible to her was the fact that Diana scorned the most beautiful riding outfits imaginable, and instead went about wearing blue jeans!

At that moment Diana was inclined less than ever to tolerate complaints and reproaches. Jack Proust would no doubt put in his two cents' worth, too, deploring the fact that his stepdaughter's absence had coincided with a visit from his dear friend, Andrew Chamberland. It would be best to avoid a confrontation, or at the very least change into something else, before facing the inevitable.

Twenty minutes later Diana emerged from the shower, refreshed and relaxed. She was brushing her long, blond hair when a commotion in the hallway sent her rushing to the door of her bedroom. She saw her Aunt Brigitte carrying her youngest child, a sturdy boy nine months old, while her grandmother was towing a little girl of four who was chirping in a reedy voice. Bringing up the rear was Celine, Brigitte's maid, a buxom woman with a scowling expression.

This procession had been an evening tradition ever since Brigitte Robin had come to visit. Brigitte's husband was away on business, and Simone Proust had invited her to stay. Once the children had finished their dinner, they were escorted to their room this way. Diana always joined the parade; not for anything would she miss saying good-night to her little cousins, and tucking them in.

Generally this operation was accomplished smoothly. Peter was a peaceful baby who let himself be tucked in without creating any fuss, for he was usually half asleep by that time. Caroline, however, tossed her covers off twenty times until all of a sudden she fell asleep with her little bottom in the air right in the middle of her antics.

That day things were happening as usual, except that Diana's aunt and grandmother looked as gloomy as Celine. Even Caroline seemed to sense that it was no time for joking since she limited her bedtime ballet to the very minimum. As soon as the door was closed, Diana asked, "What's the matter? You both look as if you've lost your best friend!"

Her grandmother, Mrs. Faber, said nothing. Brigitte merely suggested, "Let's go into my room. Dinner won't be for a while yet. Jack and Simone are still deep in conversation in the study."

Brigitte was the epitome of charm, freshness and simplicity. She wore not a speck of makeup and chose her clothes for practicality, but she was very attractive. Her full cheeks, laughing eyes, and dazzling smile combined to radiate both spiritual and physical health. She had been a nurse before she married and still retained certain characteristics of her profession: precise gestures, frankness and the capacity for selfless devotion to others. Diana adored Brigitte and treated her like an elder sister—since there was only ten years difference in their ages—as well as her best friend.

As for Mrs. Faber, she was a sixty-year-old version of Brigitte. She had the same bright eyes, radiant complexion and an aura of health. At times, however, her face could set as hard as marble and reflect nothing but pride. Today she merely looked harassed. "Celine just gave her notice," she explained.

"And the worst of it is her reason!" continued Brigitte. "She finds the countryside boring! And we took her from an isolated farm where her parents made her slave from morning to night!"

"I think she must be in love with someone in Paris," Mrs. Faber muttered.

Diana was hardly disappointed at the news. "All the better! I don't really like her anyway. She looks as if she has a grudge against the entire world."

"That's easy for you to say! She does her work properly, and that's all we ask of her. Because of her I was able to accept your mother's invitation," Brigitte said.

"How's that?"

"To run a house like this you need quite a staff. But you only have Melanie in the kitchen and one maid. Because I was able to bring Celine, I didn't feel we'd be a burden."

"We'll find a replacement for her. We'll go to the village first thing tomorrow," said Diana optimistically.

"Simone says we don't have a chance. Especially at this time of year when there's so much work on the farms."

"But you know how mother is . . . she never really gives things much thought," Diana said. Then she asked casually, "By the way, gran, I suppose everyone was looking for me this afternoon?"

"Not that I know of."

"But our friend Chamberland did honor us with a visit?" Diana persisted.

"Yet, but it was strictly business. He and Jack locked themselves up in the study for more than two hours."

"That's a bad sign! I wonder if anything's left of this place after such a long session!"

Although she did her best to adopt a bantering tone of voice, Diana could not help looking anxiously and questioningly into her grandmother's eyes. Mrs. Faber answered, "We'll probably soon find out—that is, if your parents take us into their confidence."

Then she added without a trace of bitterness, "Personally, I'm not counting on it. Your mother cut herself off from me quite a while ago."

Brigitte, who was hanging something up in the closet, turned around. "That's exactly the impression I have. I feel as if there was a break between Simone and me at some point. It's like being in a movie theater and having the sound go dead. You can watch the people on the screen, but you can't hear a word they're saying."

"And if the difficulty isn't corrected," said Diana, continuing the analogy, "the film becomes incomprehensible. . . . That's exactly what's happening here! Brigitte, I wish *someone* could tell me what the two of them are cooking up—or should I say the three of them, since Chamberland is mixed up in this!"

Mrs. Faber replied enigmatically, "You're right; he's someone to be reckoned with."

Diana was immediately on the alert. "Do you know anything, gran?"

"No, darling, and I'm not trying to discover anything. You know how I hate to pry. But I can't help thinking. . . . And I can't help worrying about you."

"Why me?"

"Well, I worry about your interests. Maybe that's the way I should put it. I know how much you love the estate and how much it would hurt you if—"

Seeing her granddaughter's terrified expression, she broke off and took Diana's face in her hands. "I said, 'if.' Remember that I don't know anything, and there's probably no reason to get upset."

"But they keep selling off—"

"Any well-run business encounters difficulties from time to time. Now don't get upset needlessly. You shouldn't worry about such things."

But the young woman broke away from her grandmother's caress.

"Don't you think it can be dangerous sometimes not to pry?" she asked, a note of irritation creeping into her voice. "I think it's almost—" she hesitated "—it's almost cowardly."

Mrs. Faber said nothing, but from the way her eyes flashed and her cheeks colored, Diana knew she had hit home. She hastened to add, "I'm sorry, gran. I don't know what's come over me. I've felt a bit lost lately. Mother doesn't tell me anything and as for Jack, he's still a stranger to me. You're the only one I can count on. And if you desert me . . . ."

Then she stopped, smiling at her aunt, "I mean you *and* Brigitte, of course! But Brigitte isn't really involved. I can't quite see her asking her sister for an account of the state of our affairs!"

Mrs. Faber seemed to be lost in thought. She remained silent for some time, gazing off into the distance as if her granddaughter's words had awakened something within her.

"You're right; you can count on me," she finally said. "I haven't done anything to clear up the situation, and it's more from cowardliness than discretion. I'm afraid I may overstep the mark and totally alienate your mother. I keep hoping she'll take me into her confidence and tell me about her problems."

Brigitte, who was usually the soul of understanding, said something that seemed out of character. "Don't worry, mother. It's probably just that their problems aren't all that serious. The day Simone really needs you . . . ."

And then immediately she turned to Diana to explain. "We're being awfully hard on your mother."

Diana tried to reassure her.

"I'm not a child anymore. I can judge people I love without having it lessen my love for them."

She had no idea, as she spoke these words, that her affection would be put cruelly to the test that very night.

Chapter 4

Dinner took place in an atmosphere that was much more relaxed than Diana had hoped for. By the time dessert was served, she had almost forgotton her earlier fears. Chamberland's visit seemed to have had no unfavorable effects on Proust's behaviour. Not only did he make no mention of Diana's absence, he behaved in an unusually friendly manner toward her.

Normally they encountered no difficulties in their relationship. They never openly disputed, but neither did they show each other any affection. Their neutrality seemed to be born of an indifference that was as mutual as it was complete.

For this reason, when Diana had cause to question herself about her stepfather, she felt not the slightest twinge of remorse.

She had discovered that she was incapable of defining or categorizing him, from either a moral or physical point of view. He was about forty-five years old, of medium height, fairly good-looking, with regular, if weak, features.

He was an easily influenced man, but no doubt an ambitious one. He had started as an accountant with Diana's father and now owned virtually everything. Perhaps there was no need to look any further for the cause of the total lack of communicaton that so surprised Diana: Proust never really concentrated on anyone but himself and therefore paid scant attention to others unless his own interests were at stake.

Diana should therefore have been on her guard that evening. Even more so since her mother appeared unusually serious as she picked at her food and obviously had to make a conscious effort to take part in the conversation.

Simone Proust was a sophisticated version of her sister, Brigitte. She was more slender and elegant—a prettier woman, but somehow less attractive. She was the sort of woman that one met at a cocktail party or saw at a fashionable hairdresser's, flipping the pages of a fashion magazine while waiting for her appointment. It was a surprise to most people meeting her for the first time, if not a shock, to discover that she was actually intelligent.

Once dinner was over, Simone usually chatted with her mother or watched television. But tonight she announced she would retire early, on the pretext that she had a migraine. But as she kissed Diana good-night she whispered in her ear, "Come and see me as soon as you can. I have to speak to you."

It was more a request than an order. Diana saw confusion in her mother's eyes and heard a slight tremor in her voice. She replied by squeezing her hand reassuringly.

Half an hour later, her heart in her mouth, Diana climbed the staircase to the second floor. Simone had not turned on the light in her room. It was bathed in shadows and for a moment Diana thought it must surely be empty.

"Come in, darling. Close the door."

She discovered her mother sitting in an armchair, looking out the window into the twilight. At the far end of the lawns, she could just make out the stable and silhouettes moving in the falling darkness, only to be swallowed by the black mouth of the stable door.

"What's the matter, mother?"

Diana leaned toward Simone a little fearfully, as if over someone wounded. Her mother's face was nothing more than a light-colored patch surrounded by blue shadows of nightfall. Nonetheless Diana could see the glittering eyes that stared directly into hers. She leaned over a little more and discovered they were full of tears.

"Are you crying?"

She asked the question with a kind of feigned indifference, for she had trained herself not to show concern or tenderness, as her mother professed complete disdain for any kind of emotional scene. Simone raised her arms and then let them sink back onto the arms of the chair.

"This isn't like me, is it? I only indulge in this kind of weakness when no one's around to see me."

Diana waited, fighting off the worry and emotion that her mother's confession inspired in her.

"Don't think it's because I'm unhappy. All things considered, I really have nothing to complain about. Still there are moments when . . . ."

Without any warning, she began to laugh. "You must wonder what all this chatter is about. I've never been a chartered accountant, but I seem to have spent the best part of the day wading through figures—"

Diana stood up, and stepped back a pace. *This is it. Finally she's going to tell me about the disaster that I've been suspecting all along,* she thought to herself.

Her mother rose and went over to a small table to turn on a lamp and flood the room with rose-colored light. Outside, night abruptly closed in around the house. Simone turned to her daughter and took her by the shoulders.

"We're the same height, but I've never really noticed it until now. When you came into the room just now, I was thinking about you. I now realize that you've crossed the barrier separating the two of us."

"What barrier?"

"The one between childhood and adulthood. The one between little girls and their mothers. I realize that you're a woman now, and that we can be friends."

"Haven't we always been?"

"No. In the sense that we each had our own little world and that there was no exchange between the two. I blame it on myself; I wanted you to stay a child forever. Today I must face the facts: you are twenty, and I have lived my best years. From now on, I can only go downhill."

Diana merely smiled, unwilling to supply the banal contradiction that her mother was fishing for. Her mother continued, "We don't have all that much time to be close to each other."

"Oh, mother, you don't believe a word of that," Diana said in mild reproach.

Once more Simone gave a small forced laugh. "No, I suppose I don't. But in any case, I want us always to be friends. Sit down next to me. You may smoke if you wish."

Diana complied, merely to have something to do. The flame of her lighter sent shadows dancing over her face.

"You have beautiful dark eyelashes, but you should take better care of your hair," Simone said, almost abstractedly.

Obviously all this commentary was no more than a prelude. But Diana accepted the situation with equanimity, although she felt a touch of disappointment at her mother's withdrawal. It was always the same: Simone let herself be caught out and seemed to weaken. But just as Diana rejoiced at the change, she would once more become the hardened society woman.

Yet tonight Diana sensed that something was different. Her mother's manner was slightly awkward and her carefree tone was forced. It was as if she was playing her usual character a little too well, and in spite of her easy comments, she continued to cry inside.

The silence stretched on interminably, but Diana was incapable of coming to Simone's aid. She sat smoking, her eyes vacant, gazing at the shaded pink lamp. She started as her mother began to speak once more.

"We can be friends, can't we? I wish it could have begun some other way. The beginning of such a relationship is something to be celebrated with champagne, music and flowers. I wish I could offer you words of happiness, but I can't. Our friendship must begin with sadness, or at least with serious problems."

Diana murmured, "I'm not really surprised."

Simone began to speak slowly and with difficulty. The prelude was finally coming to an end.

"Yes, I thought so, even though you seemed quite carefree. You understand that for some time now things haven't been going well for Jack and me. But I'm not talking about our marriage. Thank God we get along beautifully. I don't think we've ever been more aware of it than now."

From that moment on, Diana was on the defensive. She hated that sort of comment, for it dispensed so easily with her father, Alan Cavalier. Indeed, it seemed almost to be a direct insult to his memory. Her mother had re-established the distance between them, erecting a barrier infinitely more insurmountable than any age difference. Why was it that whenever Simone alluded to her second marriage, she felt the need to justify herself? No one had ever asked for any accounts!

"I've never had a moment's worry about that,"

said Diana coldly. "If Jack makes you happy, I'm the first to congratulate you."

"I know, darling. And he loves you as if you were his own daughter."

Diana refrained from comment. The statement was patently false, but in any case her stepfather's feelings for her were of little importance. Moreover, they were beside the point. Simone must have sensed her impatience, for she hastened to add, "Supposedly true friends come through when times are tough. I think the same thing can be said of love. I've always felt Jack and I were closest during difficult moments."

"Please, mother, tell me what you're driving at!"

"Well, let's just say we're having problems, financial problems."

"I see."

"But I don't want you to worry. When it comes to finances, nothing is irreparable. As a matter of fact, I decided to let you know about it tonight so that we might discuss ways to solve the problem. Because there are ways. This afternoon I discovered that you, on your own, can rectify the situation."

"Me? But how?"

"First let me explain the situation. Up until now, I've always wanted to keep you out of this sort of thing. I wanted you to remain carefree for as long as possible. But in a year you'll be twenty-one, and my guardianship will be over. I want you to help us save our fortune."

Diana felt herself going white. "Is it threatened, then?"

"Much more than you know. And it has been for

quite some time. Since your father's death and even before then. But don't think I hold him responsible. I'm not one of those people who blame whoever isn't around to defend himself. But the facts remain . . . ."

She spoke without a trace of emotion, as if she were talking about a stranger. At that moment Diana almost hated her.

"There were facts that came as a disagreeable surprise when I took over. You can imagine how I felt; I knew nothing about the business and I thought it was doing splendidly. I had no idea there was even the most minor problem. Poor Alan never told me anything. Of course, I must admit that I was young then, and my opinion wouldn't have been much help. Still, I might have been able to advise him to be cautious, and warn him about investing too heavily."

"Investing in what?"

"Just before he took sick he decided to order new machines and build new workshops. At that time, the mill was working at full capacity and he felt he didn't have enough equipment. Future prospects seemed favorable, especially with the extension of the Common Market. Do you remember how we used to go and visit the construction site to see how the work was progressing?"

It had become a tradition. Every Sunday they would make a detour to visit the factory. Diana could remember her father, bareheaded, rain or shine. Eyes sparkling, he would describe how it would look when finished. Then, one Sunday, he complained of a dreadful headache. . . .

"But in order to go into something of that scope, you have to have a solid foundation, which wasn't the case. I don't mean we didn't have any reserves, just that your father thought a little too big. And then, two important orders slipped through his fingers. When he fell ill, he wasn't able to correct the situation. To make a long story short, when he died we were almost bankrupt. If we hadn't found certain investors . . . ."

Simone leaned over toward her daughter and took her by the hand.

"You must have thought poorly of me, like everyone else. To remarry so quickly, as if I wanted to erase the memory of your father. But I don't think it was selfish of me. You have to understand how I felt at the time. I was alone. Up until then I had always been pampered and carefree. And then suddenly there were all sorts of problems to be dealt with. I felt as if I were a child, lost in the forest. You just can't understand how much someone's presence and friendship mean at times like that. Jack immediately offered to help and showed how competent he was."

She fell silent and Diana was loath to interrupt her.

"I've always been proud. I never wanted to have to account to anyone, even my own mother. Before he died, your father handed me the reins of the business. Perhaps he could see something under my frivolous exterior. I did my best, Diana, but without Jack's advice, I never would have come through it."

She hestitated a moment before going on to explain, "Without his advice and the financial help of our friend Andrew Chamberland."

Diana's eyes opened wide with surprise.

"He was helping us even then?"

"He was a business acquaintance of Jack's, and his

friend, too. Did you know he was a chartered accountant who worked for several companies as a financial advisor? Without his knowledge and money, the factory would have closed ten years ago. We should be extremely grateful to him!"

"No doubt there was more to it than friendship? Andrew doesn't strike me as being particularly philanthropic."

"Of course not. But just the same, he took considerable risks, and even now . . . ."

"Now?"

"It's hard to explain. I don't really understand it all myself. I only know that without him . . . ."

"In other words, he calls the shots?"

"Yes, in a sense. If he ever decided to withdraw his support . . . ."

"You mean that he's the real owner of the Cavalier business?"

"Not exactly. We still own most of the shares, but . . . . Anyway, we have no choice! Jack can explain it all better than I can. It's better to be at the mercy of a friend than a bank."

"Now I understand why we've been selling off the forest to him."

"We made so little money from that, anyway. And, far from giving us any advantages, the Common Market dealt us a terrible blow. Foreign competition, especially from the Germans, turned out to be more than we could match. We had to lower our prices as much as possible. And our equipment is both outdated and inefficient."

"But you're contradicting yourself. Just now you told me that father thought *too* big."

"Yes and no. It would have been better to stay where we were with limited expenses. Now we fall into the category of medium-sized businesses, the ones that are most in jeopardy."

"And . . . ?"

"We're at the same point we were ten years ago. Except that now we may not have Chamberland with us."

"Does he intend to drop us?"

"Put yourself in his place. In spite of his friendship, he can't go on losing money indefinitely. For the last ten years he hasn't received any salary or dividends."

"But he seems to have acquired an impressive amount of land!"

"Compared to his investments, it's worth very little, I assure you."

Silence fell between them. The cold unexpected words swam around in Diana's head without her being able to make any sense of them. One thought, however, dominated all others: the situation was far more serious than she had imagined even in her most pessimistic moments. From her mother's explanation, it seemed circumstances alone were to blame, since everyone had done his best. Jack Proust had furnished his efforts, Chamberland his money.

By now the sky was sparkling with stars. The curtains billowed in a fresh breeze that brought with it the fragrant odor of freshly cut hay. Diana got up and went over to the window. The night was pitch-black. She could just make out a square of light coming from her stepfather's office.

A shooting star plummeted through the sky. She smiled bitterly. Now was the time to make a wish!

She went back over to her mother and stood behind her with her hands on her shoulders. Simone asked almost timidly, "Are you sorry I took you into my confidence?"

"I would have found out sooner or later. But didn't you say just now that there was some way I could help out?"

Simone turned and took her daughter's hands, obliging her to draw closer.

"You could save us. And that's the most difficult part of what I have to tell you."

"I don't quite understand."

"If only you did!" She drew Diana to her side.

"More than ever, we have to speak as two friends, in absolute confidence. You know the problem—"

"Yes, but the solution . . . ."

"It's not really all that difficult to imagine. One can never go back, therefore one must go forward."

"Meaning?"

"At the moment, the business is not profitable. Our production costs are too high, and we can't possibly compete with foreign manufacturers. In order to lower our prices, we need modern machinery. In other words, a new influx of capital. This time we're really in trouble. We have to think really big or simply give up. Which is exactly the way Chamberland put it this afternoon when he brought us up-to-date. But he can still help us."

"So?"

"Unfortunately, he doesn't want to. He gave us to understand that he didn't want to pour any more money into us. Unless, of course . . . ."

Diana could see an anguished questioning expression in her mother's eyes. Simone knew that there was no need to finish the sentence. They remained in tense silence for several seconds, as if able to read each other's mind, then, with something like a shrug, Diana looked away.

"I see," she murmured. "I don't think you need to go on. So. It isn't just money Chamberland is talking about?"

Simone looked relieved. Her face lighted up. "I'm delighted you've caught on."

"You give me too much credit," said Diana. "When you said I could save the day, I didn't think you were referring to my financial expertise. After all, it's no secret how Chamberland feels about me." She lighted a cigarette nervously. "So what started out as a business conversation has turned into a soap opera! And I always thougt that love had nothing to do with money. Don't you find this all a little ridiculous?"

"Listen to me, Diana. Try to be objective and reasonable. Chamberland is a friend of Jack's. He confided in him and told him that he loves you. His one desire is to marry you."

"But he barely knows me!"

"Enough to appreciate and love you. I sensed it today when he was talking about you. His usual assurance was replaced by a sort of timidity. His awkwardness was touching. His voice, even his face, were different. He made me think of a schoolboy in love."

"But that doesn't deprive him of his business instincts. It doesn't stop him from talking about my love and his money in the same breath," Diana replied coolly.

"I realize that there is something slightly distasteful about this . . . this—"

"This deal! That's what it is, isn't it? If I agree to marry Chamberland, the business gets the capital it needs. If I refuse, we'll be ruined overnight."

"Now let's not exaggerate. Chamberland didn't put it that way. But it's obvious that if he can't hope for anything from you, he'll definitely pull out."

"That's exactly what I said. According to you, this 'gentleman,' is madly in love with me, but doesn't care a bit about my feelings for him. If I pretend to love him, everything will be fine. Otherwise . . . ."

Simone shook her head indulgently.

"Poor darling. I was expecting this reaction. I would have been the same way at your age. When one is twenty years old, love always means a mysterious stranger. I understand how you may feel indignant and rebellious, but I assure you, such emotions will only cloud your judgment. Chamberland is a very nice man—"

"I'm willing to admit that possibility, but I'm still not interested."

"Only because you don't know him. You can't deny that he's handsome, dashing and cultured."

"As far as I'm concerned, he's the vandal who destroyed our forest."

"He'd be crushed if he heard you say that. Because he does love you, darling, and it's so wonderful to be loved."

"But only if one loves in return!"

"You're so young and naive. A woman must never give herself up completely. The essence of the game is to make a man think that she still has to be won over."

"For God's sake, mother! What a ridiculous thing to say! Love isn't a game. It's life itself," Diana cried.

"Then I won't destroy your precious illusions. In any case, I'm not asking you to love Chamberland, but simply to give him a chance. Try to get to know him. Don't dismiss him out of hand."

"But I'm not the least bit interested in getting married."

"Only because no man has yet claimed your admiration. Can you tell me for a fact that Andrew Chamberland couldn't become that man?"

"I doubt it very much," Diana replied. "I don't feel anything for him. I don't know why, but he . . . bothers me. Somehow, I could easily picture him as the villain in a movie."

"Now you're talking like a child. You want to hang on to this house and the estate, don't you? Whether you like it or not, Chamberland is the only man who can help us keep them!"

"This is right out of a melodrama!" Diana shot back heatedly. "Will the young heroine sacrifice her happiness to save the family fortune?"

"Life often imitates art. But one thing is certain: it's up to you to make the decision—either Chamberland saves us or we go bankrupt."

Simone stood up and turned on the overhead light. Diana could not help noting the symbolic import of this move. The interlude of tender intimacy was now over.

"Think it over. You know the situation. You alone have the solution."

Diana tried hard to fight back her tears. This was *her* mother discussing Diana's happiness in the tone of voice she would use to tell her about a recipe. Why wasn't she like other mothers? Why did she always have to be so cold, so impersonal?

Almost as if she read her daughter's mind, Simone said impatiently, "Now don't overreact. What we need right now is time. You don't have to throw yourself at Chamberland and marry him next week! Just let him think that perhaps, in the future . . . . I'm sure it'll be enough to keep him happy for now. All we need is time to let us get back on our feet. And you never know, you might just fall for him."

"But that's deceitful!"

"Who's saying anything about deceit! All I ask is that you not discourage him. There's nothing wrong with a little flirting. Why, when I was your age—"

Diana headed for the door. She couldn't stand this conversation any longer. With her hand on the knob, she turned and said coldly, "Very well. I'll think about it, certainly. But even if I see your point, I doubt very much I'll be capable of going through with this sordid little farce."

"Diana, listen." Simone hurried over to take her daughter's arm. "I have to tell you one more thing. After your father died, I had no intention of marrying Jack. I assure you, I wouldn't even have noticed him if we hadn't had the business in common—"

"It was only because you needed him—"

"No, let me finish! I made no promises to him. I didn't even try to attract him. I simply spent time with him, watching him live and work. And then, little by little, I felt my admiration and friendship for him grow, until one day I realized that I loved him enough to think about starting over with him."

Diana made no reply. Simone grew embarrassed and lowered her eyes. "Of course, that doesn't mean anything. It may not happen that way with Andrew. . . ."

"Of course not!"

"I'm only asking you to give it a try. It's in your best interests, as well as mine." And so she finished a conversation that started out about friendship and ended up about money.

It was only after the door closed behind her that Diana realized she hadn't even kissed her mother good-night, as she usually did.

"WELL, ANDREW, you've come a long way since the old days, heh?" The fat man's beady eyes were cold and crafty, though his thin lips stretched into a smile.

"What the hell do you want, Reynolds? And what are you doing out here?" Chamberland's voice was tight with anger. The last person he thought to meet out here in a village inn was Erich Reynolds. And among all his past associates, Reynolds was the most dangerous.

"Let's just say I've been looking up the old gang, since I, er, returned from my little trip," Reynolds said. "I ran into Smiley in Paris. You remember

Smiley, don't you? Well, Smiley had an interesting
story to tell . . . all about this wealthy businessman
who was fast becoming a prominent landowner—
pals with the aristocracy, too."

Chamberland's face had paled. *Damn!* Of all the
rotten luck. He thought he had covered his tracks so
well. "So?" he snapped.

"So I decided to go and look up this old friend of
mine—to sort of congratulate him."

Chamberland's eyes were steely. "Let's cut out the
garbage, Reynolds. Say what you have to say, then
get out of here!"

Reynolds eased back in his chair. It creaked under
the strain of his weight. "If I didn't know better,
Andrew, I'd say you were trying to get rid of me.
Now, that couldn't be right, could it?"

Chamberland was silent for a moment. He knew
he had to do something fast for there was no telling
who might stop by and see him and Reynolds
together. He had too much at stake to risk anyone
being too curious about his acquaintances and his
past. He forced a smile. "Why, Erich, what did you
expect? You caught me off guard, that's all. Look,
let's go out for a drive. We can't talk here."
Chamberland rose and Reynolds lumbered to his
feet.

"Of course, Andrew. Only—" Reynold's hand
rested gently on Chamberland's shoulders "—Andrew, don't get cute, will you? I've made a lot of
loyal and short-tempered friends during my little
trip. They wouldn't understand if anything happened
to me."

Despite himself, Chamberland felt a shiver run down his frame.

They left the inn, and the man seated at the next table stroked his jaw thoughtfully. He had been hidden from them by a column and a large potted plant. No doubt they would have been more discreet if they had known there was someone within earshot. As it was, the young man had heard every word, and his light-colored eyes were thoughtful. "Now I wonder who those two very interesting specimens were?" he muttered to himself.

Chapter 5

Diana hestitated just outside the front door of Shady
Oaks. In the garden cicadas were buzzing in the heat
of a motionless Sunday afternoon, but a storm was
threatening. The sun had been dazzlingly bright all
morning, only to retreat behind a cover of cloud at
noonday.

She was contemplating going up to her room for a
nap—as no doubt her grandmother and Brigitte had
done directly after lunch—but she quickly rejected
the idea. It was just another way of killing time, of
putting off the decision that must be made.

Diana wandered into the garden. Her parents had
left for Rouen that morning to attend a reception
given by a doctor friend of theirs. Diana, however,
had preferred the peace and quiet of the estate rather
than the company of strangers.

Just as she was getting into the car, her mother had
said casually, "Chamberland might come over this
afternoon. I hope you'll be here to greet him."

Ostensibly it was a casual comment, but Diana knew it was heavy with significance. What Simone had really meant was, "We hope you've thought it over and decided to take the only intelligent course."

Since their conversation three days earlier, Simone had been discreet—or perhaps wise—enough not to make the slightest allusion to the problem they had discussed. No doubt she hoped that after her first indignant reaction, Diana would see the light and adopt the tactic her mother had suggested. Or perhaps she simply feared to provoke her daughter's anger and meet with an unconditional refusal.

Diana was completely undecided. In vain she had examined the situation from every angle. The banal and brutal dilemma remained: if she showed an interest in Chamberland she would be betraying every principle she believed in. If she didn't—she would destroy everything her ancestors had worked for.

It seemed that if she let the family fortune slip away, she would be betraying her father's memory. With the stakes so high, was her duty not to put her feelings aside and come to terms with reality?

If only she were trained for something—anything. She could have found a job somewhere to help keep the business going. But no, all the expensive private schools had taught her was to translate Latin and behave like a lady.

Diana gritted her teeth. Why hadn't she thought about the future? Had she hoped to remain a child forever? Now, even if she managed to become sufficiently trained for some job, it would not help her family. Too little, too late.

Diana crossed the kitchen garden. The motionless

foliage looked like steel under the white light.
Peonies and four-o'clocks bent their parched leaves
to the ground. No sound was to be heard, save the
lazy clucking of the chickens and the distant carillon
announcing the beginning of Vespers in the village.

She passed behind the stables, and it occurred to
her to saddle Prince. But then she took pity on her
old companion. It would be unkind to impose a long
walk on him in the heat and the buzzing flies. Neither
was she tempted by the prospect of having to glance
at her watch every few minutes in order to be back
when Chamberland . . . . She was surprised to catch
herself thinking such thoughts. Perhaps unconsciously she had made her decision to accept his attentions?

She would see him, but no more than that. In her
parents' absence she was obliged to act as lady of the
house. In no way would she compromise herself.
Perhaps the wisest course was simply to relax and see
what would happen, as Brigitte had advised her.

In her distress, Diana had chosen her aunt and not
her grandmother as her confidante, for fear that the
older woman might interfere. Anyway, Brigitte was
younger and closer to her. It had been easier to talk
to her. To say with feigned lightheartedness, "Do
you know what's happened? They've put me up for
sale to save the furniture! Chamberland apparently
wants to buy me!"

This conversation had taken place the day before
on the way back from the village, where they had
tried in vain to find a replacement for Celine. Brigitte
was driving her little car more nervously than usual.
The brittle expression on her niece's face caused her
to slow down for a talk.

"Yes! I hold the fate of four people in my hands. I'm worth a factory, a house, a stable, seven farms and one thousand acres of Normandy."

"Personally, I think you're worth a bit more than that. But why put this value on yourself?" Brigitte asked.

As Diana began to relate the conversation with her mother, Brigitte pulled off onto a side road and stopped the car. With the roof open and the windows down, in the fresh, green countryside, the facts she related seemed much less ominous than they had in her mother's shadowy bedroom. She was even able to discuss it casually.

When Diana had finished, Brigitte commented, "I'm not a bit surprised. It's obvious that Chamberland is in love with you. I've only seen him two or three times, but from the way he looks at you and the way his behavior changes the minute you walk into the room—"

"His feelings for me are beside the point. I'm talking about the way I feel about him!"

"At the moment you don't feel anything for him, so you don't have to make any decision."

"Mother wants—"

"She wants you not to turn your back on him. She wants you to contemplate talking to him and spending some time together. You don't have to look beyond that first step. But if you don't take that first step, you won't know anything will you?"

"That means you think I should—"

"Look, you don't have to turn on the charm the minute he walks in the door, but you don't have to rush off and hide in the forest, either. Just be yourself

with him, pretend there is no question of money
underlying your relationship. Even if you couldn't
and wouldn't marry him for money, it would be a
serious mistake to brush him aside, because he could
help you."

Brigitte was right. Diana knew she could rely on
her common sense and objectivity. But even if she
did come to feel something for Chamberland, money
would still be in the background, irreparably spoiling
the relationship before it had even begun.

Diana left the garden and crossed the meadow in
front of the old orangery. Beside the orangery itself,
which had been empty for many years, was a tiny
house that had once been the home of a gardener. It
was a thatched house with clay walls, beamed ceiling
and tiny windows, and neatly surrounded by shrubs
and flowers.

It had always been one of Diana's favorite spots.
As a little girl she would spend entire afternoons in its
one room, raising a family of countless dolls and
overseeing an impressive collection of stuffed
animals. Later she had used it as a study when she
was preparing for final exams.

Even now she still returned fairly often to read or
knit, unconsciously obeying some mysterious law
that causes young girls who live in mansions to
dream of thatched houses, and young girls who live
in thatched houses . . . .

Opening the Dutch door, Diana stood stock-still
one step inside the room, surprised not to discover
the usual aroma of apples and old wood. Some
aroma she could not quite define was floating in the air.

She took another step or two, breathed in deeply, and looked around blinking after the dazzling light of outdoors. Suddenly she started at the sound of a voice coming from the far end of the room.

"Hello, again."

She recognized the mocking voice instantly, and it caused her to pale with emotion and surprise. She stood immobile and speechless, as if an invisible hand were clutching at her throat. At the same time she realized that the unusual odor came from the tobacco of his cigarette.

Diana could barely make him out in the scant light as he began to speak once again in familiar nonchalant tones.

"Come in. You're not disturbing me at all. I had just finished a little siesta and I was thinking about you. I was imagining that you would appear in the doorway and come toward me offering your most charming smile. Definitely a premonition."

The expression on Diana's face, however, could scarcely be decribed as a smile. Lips tightly drawn together and nostrils trembling, she stared at the young man. But just as the first time they met, he seemed not the slightest bit disconcerted.

"Sit down. I'm sorry I can't offer you anything, but won't you sit down?" He pushed a chair forward. "This isn't the most comfortable chair, but after all, we are in the country, aren't we?" Then he smiled disarmingly, his face lighting up.

Despite herself, Diana felt her initial wave of anger wearing off. Ignoring the chair, she said, "Listen, Mr.—"

"Please, call me Paul. It's my first name, and I'm very fond of it. What's yours?"

Without thinking she said, "Diana."

Paul nodded. "It suits your blond hair and peaches-and-cream skin. I'm sure we'll get along splendidly."

Diana finally managed to mutter in a strangled voice, "Who said you could come in here?"

"No one. I didn't come across anyone on my way here." And then with that same disarming smile, he added, "And since I didn't see any signs, either . . . ."

But Diana had no desire to be disarmed. She gave a short derisive laugh that did not quite ring true and then said, "Since you attach so little importance to signs, I doubt they would have discouraged you, anyway."

"You judge me so harshly. But then, children often make snap decisions."

"How dare you! Only a few days ago I found you swimming in my favorite pond, in the middle of our estate, ignoring God knows how many warning signs. And not only were you not the least bit embarrassed, not only did you not offer any apology, you openly made fun of me. In fact, you were quite rude."

Paul assumed an ingenuous and surprised expression.

"Another misunderstanding. I was only trying to inject a little humor into the situation."

"Oh, I know. You think you're so funny. You have such an inflated opinion of yourself."

"Hardly inflated—"

"And now I find you in this house, which has always meant a great deal to me."

"Where should I go to avoid you? Is is my fault you own the entire countryside?"

"No I don't own the entire countryside! There are lots of other houses in the village—why didn't you pick one of them?"

"I'll tell you why: most of them are occupied by nice people but whose acquaintance I have no desire to make. Besides, I like peace and quiet, so this cool little thatched house suits me to a T."

"Ah, you admit that you broke in."

"I walked in; the door was open."

"And you made yourself at home. You took a nap on the bed, and you put your books on the table so they'd be in easy reach."

"You've got to admit it would have been stupid of me to lie down on the ground and put my books on top of the wardrobe."

"Of course, what am I thinking of! I just can't understand why it surprises me so." If he could be sarcastic, so could she.

"Now you're catching on! I was sure you'd end up admitting—"

"I admit only that you have a strange way of looking at things. And that's an understatement! I'm beginning to wonder if you're responsible for your actions!"

"You underestimate me. My behavior is the result of undeniable logic."

Diana was angry at herself for letting the conversation continue, but she had no idea how to end it. She was tempted to turn on her heel and stalk out, slamming the door behind her, but that would only be a second admission of defeat. She also had to admit that even though it exasperated her, this debate was an almost welcome departure from her usual worries.

Moreover, her opponent did have a certain something. He was about thirty years old and not quite as tall as she'd thought at the pond. His features were roughly hewn and his skin darkly tanned. She could not quite make out the color of his clear eyes, but there was no missing their mischievous sparkle. Then she noticed his sunburnt peeling nose and felt an unmistakable twinge of tenderness.

Diana sank into the chair he had proffered only minutes earlier. Chin resting on her hand, she sat staring at the floor with a look of resignation on her face.

"Poor little rich girl," Paul said, almost tenderly. "Wealth implies certain obligations, doesn't it? I've lived long enough to realize that the majority of people do not own, but rather are owned. I've even come to believe that you can enjoy something even more if it doesn't belong to you. Take your pond, for example. If I owned it, I probably wouldn't have the slightest desire to swim in it. Or this house. I'd probably just rent it or sell it."

Diana looked up. Finally she had found an opening in his torrent of words.

"I'm in complete disagreement with you and your fine theories. I happen to own this house, and I *do* enjoy it. And if you would be so kind as to leave, I could enjoy it even more."

"I salute your unusual ability to enjoy what you own. But we'll see how you feel twenty years from now."

That one sentence was enough to plunge Diana back into the depths of her problems. Forgetting momentarily that she had resolved to remain on the defensive, she could not help murmuring, "In twenty years I may own nothing."

There was a short silence during which her eyes met Paul's. She was surprised by the serious attentive look on his face. She felt herself blushing and angrily lowered her eyes. But to her great relief, he asked no questions, but merely continued in the same offhand tone.

"The problem is that I've inherited certain tastes that don't quite go along with my meager resources. I love wide open spaces, solitude and independence. I also like the homes and furniture of what I call old France. And that's why I'm irresistibly attracted to private property. It's the only place where I really feel at home."

Diana stood up, her voice accusatory once again. "In short I should consider myself lucky not to have found you in my bedroom? It's easy to follow your line of reasoning; you're a parasite!"

"Wrong word. A parasite lives at someone else's expense. I never impose on anyone, nor do I ask anyone for anything. Personally, as long as I have peace and quiet—"

"On someone else's property."

"Simply because it's hard to find it elsewhere. So, I just had to come to your place!"

"Impeccable logic. You're too lazy to earn a living, but you want to enjoy the advantages money brings."

Paul frowned in concentration and then replied, "That's just about it. But 'lazy' isn't quite the right word. Occasionally I work when I can't avoid it. But then again, it depends on the way you interpret the word. For example, writing a poem or an article on a subject that interests me does not fall into the category of work."

Once again there was a short silence. Their eyes met, Paul's mocking, Diana's fairly flashing sparks. She knew she was fighting a losing battle. She sensed with growing awareness that she was no match for Paul's repartee. Minute by minute, she lost hope of being able to have the last word. It was obvious, however, that Paul was having a fine time, like a cat playing with a mouse. He even went so far as to say, in complete seriousness, "Now that you understand me, admit that our meetings are somehow symbolic. They prove we have the same tastes, and love the same things—the pond, this house—"

"They don't prove anything except your boorishness! And I certainly hope that this is the last example of it."

Paul's voice dropped almost to a whisper. "It doesn't depend on me. Up until now, it's been you who's come to me."

"You're unbelievable! I suppose you expect me to apologize to you."

"Of course not. The lady of the manor doesn't apologize to the peasant."

Diana no longer even tried to save face, for she was consumed by anger, and searched for something scathing to shoot back at him. But all she could do was stammer, "I . . . I . . . I hate you!"

"I doubt that. If you agreed to get to know me better . . . ."

Later, when she looked back on the conversation, Diana wondered how she had resisted the temptation to slap his face, for his gently mocking smile had goaded her beyond measure.

Suddenly she decided she'd had enough. She got up and made for the door. It was time to retreat, for her eyes were beginning to fill with tears. Exasperation, nervous tension and the feeling of sorrow that had been at the back of her mind for the past few days all contributed to her breaking down.

In her haste to leave, she stumbled in the doorway and almost lost her footing. With surprising quickness Paul was at her side, his hands steadying her. The touch of his firm brown fingers on the bare flesh of her upper arm produced a completely unfamiliar sensation to Diana. *Why it's like a shock and a shiver all at once,* she thought in surprise.

For a moment she was so taken aback by her senses and her thoughts, she offered little resistance when Paul slowly turned her to him. Wide-eyed, Diana stared at the firm well-shaped mouth irrevocably descending on hers, almost as if she were mesmerized. Her eyes were still open when the kiss came. She did not know at what point she closed them in delicious surrender.

Diana had been kissed occasionally before, but

nothing had prepared her for this experience, this blossoming of senses within her. She felt herself clinging to Paul, pulling him closer. In response Paul's kiss deepened, became more urgent.

Unprepared for her first taste of passion, Diana panicked. With a gasp she broke free of Paul's arms, then with a muffled cry she ran through the door.

"Diana!"

But the moment was lost. Fearing that he might follow her, she began to run through the tall grass toward the orchard.

Hands in his pockets, Paul watched her go with a bemused look on his face. Long after she disappeared, he still stood pensively in the doorway of the house. After closing the door he frowned, stretched out on the wooden bed, and picked up his book with a sigh.

Two hours later, his jacket slung over one shoulder, Paul was strolling along the road to the village, whistling a tune as he went. Suddenly a blaring horn caused him to jump to one side. A huge red convertible swept by, leaving him in a cloud of dust. He saw Diana, her hair waving in the wind, flash by without so much as a sideways glance. The man at the wheel appeared to be debonair and slender and was dressed in an expensive gray suit.

The car disappeared. Paul stopped walking, but continued whistling softly. For a good minute he stood by the side of the road, lost in thought. Then he turned around and set off back toward Shady Oaks.

Chapter 6

Although she was usually an early riser, Diana slept late the next morning. She was vaguely displeased with herself—a feeling exacerbated by a nagging headache that reminded her of all the wine and rich food she had consumed the night before when she had gone out to dinner with Andrew.

Now that some time had elapsed, she felt anything but proud of her date with Chamberland. She'd put herself out to be charming and flirtatious. It was impossible not to chastise herself for what she had done. But not for a moment would she admit that her friendliness toward Chamberland had been an act of defiance—a result of her interlude with Paul.

Paul. For a moment Diana traced the pattern of her lips with her fingertips, reliving that searing kiss. What was Paul doing today, she wondered. Had he continued on his way, perhaps thinking in amusement about the silly little girl he'd flirted with, who had panicked and run away? At the thought, hot flames of embarrassment burned Diana's cheeks. Suddenly angry with herself, she forced her thoughts back to Chamberland. He had been a charming and courteous escort, but the thought of his even kissing her filled her with distaste.

Diana rubbed a hand across her aching forehead. *Oh, what have I let myself in for,* she wondered. *I told Brigitte I'd never marry him, and yet I've agreed to see him again. I'm leading him on. I'm manipulating him, and it's all so calculated. I'm ashamed of myself.*

A shower and two aspirins made her feel a bit better. As she strolled over to the stable to ask that Prince be saddled for an afternoon ride, she tried to rationalize her behavior.

When it comes right down to it, our relationship is well defined—simple friendship, and that's all.

But everything was thrown back into question at lunch, when her mother kissed her with unusual affection and said, "Jack just called me from the factory. Andrew came to see him this morning before he left for the Continent. He told him what a good time the two of you had together last night."

Because her grandmother walked into the room at that very moment, Diana merely gestured vaguely in reply. But during the meal, she found herself harboring fresh reasons for resentment.

That telephone call is like some kind of report. He's letting her know that I played my role properly. A lollipop for the little girl who did what she was told.

During her entire ride in the woods, Diana couldn't banish these thoughts from her mind. Even Prince didn't quite seem up to form; several times he almost stumbled and he hung his head as if weighed down.

And yet the heat of the preceding day had abated. It had rained during the night and the air held the fragrance of toadstools and freshly washed leaves. But above the trees the gray sky stretched unrelieved, giving the forest shadows an almost liquid quality.

Diana wisely avoided Templars' Crossing, knowing it was definitly not the time to confront her ravaged forest. She took a shortcut to the pond, using a service path that was barely discernible among the timber, thinking sadly that this new route was yet another proof of how her domain had shrunk in size. In the future perhaps even the pond would no longer be part of the estate.

She felt as if everything was conspiring to feed the fires of her sorrow. She wondered how she had ever thought she might recapture the old joy that such rides had once inspired. The familiar trees and bushes seemed frozen in the harsh light, as if waiting for their destiny to be decreed. Even the pond seemed to greet her with a large question mark.

This time—thank goodness—there was no one there. As she was wont to do, Diana settled down on the little platform formed by the sluice gate.

Her thoughts went to Paul. There was one good thing about this stranger: he distracted her from the vicious circle that her thoughts had been following for the past few days. He was a sort of tonic. He made her nervous, but at this point even that was far

preferable to sorrow. Paul was an excellent counter-
irritant!

Diana could not repress a smile when she thought
of him. At least he, for one, had no ulterior motives.

"The majority of people do not own, but rather are
owned. . . ."

He might as well have been referring to Diana
herself. Was it not true that all her unhappiness
stemmed from the very things that should have made
her happy? Paradoxically enough, was she not on the
point of giving up what she held dearest so that she
might be able to keep her happiness?

Paul, on the other hand, seemed to be poor. Yet he
also seemed to be happy. Diana realized that it was
perhaps this quality that so exasperated her when she
was with him. His carefree happiness somehow ig-
nited a spark of jealousy in her.

For a long time she sat pensively, gazing at the
reflections on the surface of the pond. The all-
pervasive silence, combined with the greenery
reflected in the immense mirror, had an almost
trancelike effect on her. Her thoughts melted away to
be replaced by a vague torpor.

But the distant noise of a motor effectively shattered her reverie. No doubt it was a tractor on the
other side of the crossing, coming to drag away the
fallen trees.

Diana stood up, mounted her horse, and began to
ride back to the house. If she didn't dawdle, she
would arrive in time to see the children put to bed.
They at least loved her and meant her no harm.

IT WAS DECIDEDLY an unlucky day, for even that one small joy was to be refused her.

The house was quiet. Melanie, the cook, was peeling vegetables on the steps of the pantry and begrudgingly offered replies to Diana's questions.

"But you know very well that Mrs. Proust went to Elbeuf to meet Mr. Proust!"

Diana either had not known or had forgotten. Her parents had gone out to a dinner party again. But, in fact, they went out so often that she was more surprised when they stayed at home. Melanie, however, tended to interpret things in her own way, which usually was not terribly optimistic.

"Probably they don't like my cooking!"

Today she was particularly cranky.

Diana tried another subject. "Where are the children?"

"The children? Do you think I have the time to keep track of them, too?"

Then she added an enigmatic comment that ostensibly had no relation with what had gone before. "And you can bet that I won't, either!"

Diana thought it best to drop the matter without asking for any explanation, and decided to go up to her room to change.

She stopped in the hall with a frown on her face, for she could hear a vacuum cleaner start up in her aunt's bedroom.

Diana frowned. *I thought Celine quit this morning. And, anyway, this isn't the time of day for cleaning.*

Curiosity overcame her and she opened the door. Her hand on the knob, she stopped dead in her tracks at the sight of Paul wearing a long blue apron like those worn by café waiters.

Diana's eyes grew wide and she stood frozen in stunned silence. At the sight of her, Paul promptly shut off the machine and nodded respectfully.

"May I be of service?"

There was not even a hint of a smile on his face and his mocking manner had been replaced by icy deference. After a few seconds Paul said, "No doubt you are surprised by my presence here. I understand completely. I should explain that since this morning I have been in Mrs. Robin's employ. . . ."

Then he went on to explain more fully, "Mrs. Robin, who is, I believe, your aunt. I am replacing Celine."

His speech gave Diana time to gather her thoughts and pull herself together. When she finally spoke it was in a calm tone of voice.

"I suppose this is some kind of joke."

"Please let me assure you that a joke is the farthest thing from my mind. Mrs. Robin seems to attach a great deal of importance to household matters. Moreover, she struck me as an extremely competent person. Otherwise, I never would have accepted her offer."

"She . . . offered you . . . ?"

"Yes . . . and no. Since you seem interested, I should perhaps tell you how things came about. I hope you won't mind if I dust the furniture as I explain?"

As he spoke, Paul began to vigorously polish a chest of drawers.

"Not too long ago, I became acquainted with Fernand Calouche, your gatekeeper. When I passed by his home a couple days ago, Fernand happened to mention the problems you've been having with servants. At the time I paid almost no attention to the remark. But only yesterday, I got the idea of applying for a job. So I went to see Mrs. Robin. And this morning I moved my things from the inn in the village to Celine's room. And that's that."

"And how long do you plan to continue this ridiculous farce?"

"The fact that you use the term 'farce' shows that you totally misunderstand my intentions. Moreover, the word 'farce' could scarcely be used to describe the amount of work to be done in this house."

His expression was impassive, his tone devoid of irony. His voice conveyed just the right nuance of respect. He made no allusion to their previous meetings—for which Diana should have been glad. But for some reason, she found his measured, almost dignified manner exasperating.

"Then I was right yesterday when I made that comment about finding you in my bedroom!"

Paul stopped dusting. "Mrs. Robin didn't say anything about that. But, of course, I'm at your service whenever my other duties are completed."

Diana bit her lip, flushed crimson, and realized that the fingers of her right hand were stiff from gripping the doorknob.

"Fine! I've a good mind to go straight to my aunt and tell her exactly what I think of all this!"

"I take it you don't approve?"

Paul asked this question with almost complete equanimity, as if the answer mattered little to him. At the same time he stepped back and cocked a critical eye at the chest of drawers he had just polished. Once satisfied that it met with his approval, he started on the second chest of drawers, and without waiting for any answer went on talking.

"I would be most upset, because I like this house very much and hope to live here in complete harmony with all its occupants. However, I do foresee some problems with Melanie. . . ."

Diana suddenly realized why the cook had been so grumpy; she liked to rule the entire household with uncontested authority and had probably found out that Paul could not be bullied.

"Thank goodness I won't have to go into the kitchen," Paul continued. "Except, of course, to prepare the children's meals. That reminds me . . . . I do hope you'll excuse me. . . ."

He glanced at his watch. "Caroline and Peter will soon be back from their walk. I must prepare their dinner and get them ready for bed."

The room was sparkling clean. Paul contemplated his work, then added a few finishing touches. He straightened a picture frame, went over two or three spots with his duster, put the armchairs back in their usual places, and unplugged the vacuum cleaner. His gestures were precise and completely natural. Diana stood rooted to the spot watching him. She was at a loss for words but couldn't quite tear herself away from the scene. Luckily, he refrained from looking at her.

Then he picked up his equipment and stepped past her out into the hall without a backward glance.

A tight-lipped Diana did an about-face and stalked off in the opposite direction.

"WHAT'S GOING ON? Did you really hire him to replace Celine?"

"Of course I did. Why do you look so shocked?" Brigitte replied.

"How could you? It's ridiculous—"

"What's wrong with it? I'm surprised at you. Everybody else thinks he's a godsend!"

"Oh, they do, do they? Why don't you ask Melanie how she feels about it?"

"Melanie only thinks of herself. I didn't think it necessary to ask for her opinion."

"Does mother know about this?" Diana persisted.

"Of course. She gave me carte blanche to hire whomever I wished."

Mrs. Faber spoke up at this point, trying diplomatically to smooth things over. "In any case, dear, we have no choice. We needed someone right away, and you know how hard it is to find a maid at this time of year."

The conversation was taking place in the park. Diana had gone to meet her aunt and grandmother, who were strolling back toward the house.

Caroline had put up a struggle to be allowed to push her brother's carriage without any grown-up help. Each time the carriage swerved and her mother reached out to straighten its course she would protest. Chubby Peter enjoyed every minute, laughing delightedly each time his pram tipped at a precarious angle.

"Why didn't you tell me anything about it?" Diana asked.

"We weren't sure it would actually happen until he arrived with his suitcase. And, to tell you the truth, it didn't even cross our minds. Besides, you were hardly in the mood for conversation at lunchtime!" Brigitte replied.

"I'm sure you'll regret it."

"In any case, he's doing a marvelous job so far. He did as much work in two hours this afternoon as Celine would have done in two days," Brigitte said admiringly.

"We'll see. If you ask me, he's nothing but an impostor!"

"How do you know? Do you know him already?"

Diana felt her color rising and grew furious at herself.

"Yes. . . . I've come across him once or twice. Last week he was swimming in the pond, and yesterday I found him in the little thatched house."

Mrs. Faber smiled. "I know. Paul was very frank about confessing that he'd met you already."

Diana colored. *I'll bet he didn't tell you everything*, she thought.

"No doubt he omitted to mention the offhand way he treated me?" she said.

"Was he rude to you?" Brigitte queried.

"Well, not in the usual sense of the word, but—"

"Did he say anything disparaging?"

"Not really. It was more his attitude . . . his insolence . . . ."

"I'm surprised. He gave us the impression of being extremely polite. Didn't he, mama?" she said, turning to Mrs. Faber.

"But he just walked in and took over that little house."

"Fernand gave him the idea. He wanted to be able to read and work in peace, and since the inn where he was staying is as noisy as a zoo all day—"

"Fernand must be getting senile. He's forgotten that his job is to chase vagrants away, not welcome them with open arms."

"Now, now, you don't really mean that. Usually you're so much more understanding. I'm sure you'll have second thoughts."

"I doubt it very much! I don't relish the prospect of locking horns day after day with someone who's always trying to make a fool of me."

"Oh, come now, Diana, I think you're exaggerating. From now on he'll be working for us, and I'm sure he'll play his role properly," Brigitte said soothingly.

"Well, we'll just wait and see whether—"

Diana broke off when a man appeared on the steps. But it took her several seconds to be sure that it was Paul. Once again he was changed in appearance. This time he was wearing a white smock that made him look like a surgeon.

Even Mrs. Faber and Brigitte were taken aback. He replied to their puzzled expressions with a half smile playing about his lips.

"For the children's baths," he said formally.

This was in reference to Caroline and Peter, who blithely overlooked Paul's formal approach.

Caroline, for her part, showed complete and utter disdain for decorum by immediately releasing Peter's baby carriage, and using her sturdy legs to jump all social barriers, threw herself into the young man's arms.

"You're handsome!" she crowed. "Can I kiss you?"

"If your mother does not mind. . . . "

Brigitte was rather embarrassed. Diana's presence and her obvious disapproval obliged her to hide her natural reaction. Ordinarily she would have smiled indulgently at such obvious evidence of love at first sight. But this time, in the severest tone of voice she could muster, she ordered, "Get down, Caroline! Leave Paul alone!"

Paul looked sympathetically at his newfound little friend, who was threatening to dissolve into tears. But he was all composure when he announced, "I'm afraid I must inform you, ma'am, that I won't be able to prepare Peter's pablum, since Melanie has forbidden me to enter the kitchen."

"I'll look after that. Thank you, Paul. That's all for tonight."

The young man bowed, hesitated, then said, "If it meets with your approval . . . I noticed that the bell connecting the corridor on the second floor to my room is broken. I'll try to repair it. That way you'll be able to call if you need me during my off hours."

TWENTY MINUTES LATER, when she went upstairs to comb her hair before dinner, Diana discovered Paul, dressed this time in a gray smock, standing on a stepladder in order to reach the wires connecting the bell.

She pretended to pay no attention to him, but couldn't help noticing that he was so absorbed in his work that he was oblivious of her.

Chapter 7

The next few days proved all of Diana's predictions to be totally inaccurate. Not only did Brigitte and Madam Faber have no reason to regret hiring Paul, they continually found new reasons to congratulate themselves for doing so.

Paul was punctual, efficient, silent and discreet. In short, he was undoubtedly a rare find—one of a species long considered extinct. He soon managed to make friends with everyone—except Diana.

Without admitting it to herself, Diana was annoyed because Paul played his role so well and managed to occupy her thoughts so often. In spite of herself, she could not help watching his every move, trying to catch him out.

Until now this pleasure had been refused her. Paul had been treating her with the same impersonal efficiency as the other members of the family. On the rare occasions when he found himself alone with her, not only did he avoid the tone of their first conversations, he was more formal and reserved than ever. It was hard to believe he had actually held her in his arms and kissed her passionately.

One night she gave in to the temptation to pierce his reserve. She ran into him at the stables, where he often went once his work was finished for the day. He was leaning on the fence, watching one of the stable hands train a yearling. Since Diana approached from one side, he didn't notice her at first. Seen in profile against the setting sun, his tanned face made her think of adventure in the great outdoors. From time to time he laughed silently when the horse refused to obey. When he finally turned and noticed Diana, the emotion left his face and his features became immobile.

"Do you need me for something?" he asked.

"No. I just wanted to see how Mikado was coming along."

Then, as she leaned against the fence, she added, "Besides, you work for my aunt."

"I'd be only too happy to perform any service for you, Miss Cavalier."

"You might as well stop calling me Miss Cavalier. You must get tired of all these linguistic acrobatics."

"Rest assured; I've always been gifted at such things."

"So I've noticed. You were a great deal less formal then."

"I had no reason to be formal.".

"You were even rather forward."

"I had no reason not to be."

Diana flushed. Was he hinting that she had encouraged him? "Really? You think it's normal to . . .

to behave as you did to someone you don't even know?"

"Of course. I'm sure you'll understand. At that time we were outside any well-defined social context. I was free, and you were a beautiful stranger."

He bowed. "Today you're just as beautiful, but unfortunately you're no longer a stranger."

"Why do you say that?"

"Because you live in a certain milieu that is far removed from mine."

"Do you find that sort of thing particularly important?"

"Me, no. Others, yes. So I pretend, so as not to upset them."

"You pretend! That's exactly what I thought. Everything you do and say is nothing more than one long act!"

"Everyone plays a role. Everyone tries to do his best in the little part that fate assigns him. Your stepfather, for example, does his best to act like the president of a company. And your mother does her best to act like a haughty, insensitive society woman—"

"How dare you!"

"And she carries it off with great ease. And as for this Mr. Chamberbun about whom I've heard a great deal—"

"Chamberland."

"This Mr. Chamberland, who plays the role of a business tycoon and a young man in love . . . . And as we all know, the two do not quite go hand in hand. He'll need a lot of talent to carry it off. And then there's you—"

"I have the feeling that you've forgotten your

role, " Diana said when Paul stopped suddenly.
"Please forgive me. But just now you were
reproaching me—".

"What were you going to say about me?"

"That you were perhaps the only one who always
remains perfectly sincere and natural. For example,
I'm convinced that at this moment you're not making
the slightest attempt to simulate anger."

The little game came to an abrupt end. Diana
proved Paul right by calling him a boor and turning
her back. Then, after a moment's hesitation, she
strode off.

Paul calmly lighted a cigarette and ᵗ ᵗᵉᵈ his attention back to the yearling.

THAT SAME NIGHT Diana was unable to sleep, so she
went over to her window to pass the time. Night
hung on her shoulders like a heavy cloak. The sky
held neither moon nor stars. Outside there was
nothing but humid shadows without a breath of air.
The tips of the trees faded into the sky. Only one
light was on, at the right side of the house, above a
curtain of shrubbery. It was the light in Paul's room.

Diana stood staring at it, recalling the details of
their latest conversation. At the same time, her
grandmother's question came back to her. "Why
aren't you nicer to him?"

She wondered why she always felt the need to be
aggressive toward Paul. Whereas in reality . . . . In
reality, what? He was interesting, and original, and
maybe even fascinating, but what of it? He was
essentially a frivolous changeable man who played
with life just as he played with words.

In two weeks or a month, he would leave the estate after exhausting the possibilities of his game and the novelty of his new role. He would perhaps go off to another family, where some other young woman would hang on to his every word.

He must think I have no sense of humor. But what does it matter anyway? I don't really care what he thinks of me!

Diana stared angrily at the tiny rectangle of light. Was it the oppressive heat or the shadows that made her breathing difficult? Or was it the thought that she was to see Chamberland again the next day . . . ?

Her brief reprieve was over, and her problems had come to the fore again. Diana felt she did not have the strength to face them. Beginning tomorrow morning, she would no longer have the right to be "sincere and natural." She would have to calculate every word and gesture. What a pity it was, at the age of twenty, to have to think of love as a disagreeable obligation, and as a result feel disgust at the very idea.

While he was away, Chamberland had written to her twice, a postcard from Milan and a letter from Istanbul. Except for the stamp and the postmark, they could have been written from anywhere. There was no mention of what he had done, nor any hint of local color.

Diana could easily imagine the way he traveled: jet plane, taxi, impressive hotel, business meetings in a glass and concrete cage in the heart of a city. In the evening, dinner—a business dinner, of course—in a fancy restaurant, and to top it off, a nightclub featuring Parisian artists on tour. . . .

Chamberland's style of writing seemed compatible with the trip. First there were classic comments— "hot . . . tired . . . but satisfactory results . . . "—and at the end, a timid attempt at sentimentality— "longing to see you again and perhaps spend more time in that little restaurant. . . ."

Of course! It was only natural that he should fit love in just as he would check an invoice or order new supplies. Paul was right; Chamberland would have a hard time playing the role of lover and financier at the same time.

The light had gone out and Diana began to feel strangely alone and disoriented. Time hung heavier, and the silence was even more oppressive.

Then, in the depths of the night, she heard a noise. Someone was brushing against the bushes and she could hear a bicycle crunching along the gravel. Then the light on the handlebars switched on and she could make out Paul's silhouette as he jumped on the bicycle. Diana automatically turned to her bedside clock; the hands showed midnight.

Where can he be going at this time of night?

For some reason the thought brought an ache to her heart. She felt suddenly that the night had grown overtly hostile toward her. Now the air seemed to be filled with the acrid odor of rotting grass. She nervously closed her shutters, pinching one of her fingers as she did so. The pain brought tears to her eyes.

Yet she was grateful for the pain that let her cry without having to make an excuse.

Chapter 8

Paul cast one last glance at the job he had just done. Then he carefully gathered up all traces of his work, closing the bookcase door and sweeping up the bits of wire and sawdust that had fallen to the floor.

His bag of tools in hand, he opened the door of the study, listened attentively, and stepped out into the hall. It was the middle of the afternoon, the hottest time of the day. As usual, everyone was either sleeping or reading in solitude. Only in the house was shady coolness to be found.

The young man went into the small living room adjacent to the study. He pulled back a wall hanging and began to unscrew a buzzer that apparently no longer worked. He took a similar-sized metal object out of his pocket, attached it to the wires in place, and screwed it into the wall where the first one had been.

Then he tidied up after himself and put away his

splicing tape and screwdriver. He stood back, looking at his work with obvious pleasure. Then he noticed Mrs. Faber standing in the doorway with a look
of surprise on her face. He started slightly and then
apologized with a smile. "You made so little noise; I
wasn't expecting—"

"Neither was I. I wanted to do some reading in
here. It's so much cooler than my room. I wasn't expecting to find you here," Mrs. Faber said
thoughtfully.

"I'm sorry."

"Are you still working?"

"If you want to call it that. Actually, repairing
things is one of my favorite pastimes, especially
anything electrical."

"Is that a socket you're working on?"

"No, it's a buzzer. There's an insane number of
them in this house. But most of them seem to be just
for show, which I'm trying to correct."

"Do you think it'll be . . . helpful?"

Paul thought the question over for two or three
seconds and then looked Mrs. Faber directly in the
eyes.

"Very helpful," he concluded seriously. "If you'll
trust me and ask no further questions for the moment, I may soon be able to prove just how useful
these can be."

With these enigmatic words, he bowed and left the
room.

Mrs. Faber sat down in an armchair near the window, but her book remained closed on her lap.

IN THE STUDY, Proust, red in the face, sat behind his desk, staring at Chamberland seated across from him. "But we agreed you'd keep the mill going for the time being."

Chamberland shrugged. *But then I didn't have that parasite Reynolds on my back*, he thought. "My dear Proust," he said, "you can't expect me to wait forever."

"This is intolerable. We made a bargain—"

"Yes," Chamberland interrupted, "but your part of the bargain is not going as smoothly as it should."

"That's not my fault," Proust blustered. "I can't force Diana to fall in love with you."

Chamberland's eyes glinted. "We weren't discussing love. We were discussing marriage."

"You swine. This situation is intolerable. But what should I expect from a crook!"

"I take exception to this word 'crook,' " Chamberland said mildly. "I'm not denying it, but coming from you I find it hardly appropriate. If you'll think back to the beginning of our friendship fifteen years ago . . . . "

Proust shrugged in exasperation. "Yes, yes, I know it all by heart! Those unfortunate commissions that I took when I was in charge of buying—"

"Unfortunate? You didn't seem so squeamish about it at that time."

"I didn't have a cent! I was making just enough to keep from starving!"

"Exactly. You should at least have been grateful that you were lodged and fed."

"Well, you certainly found enough arguments to counter my scruples!"

" 'Fear' is the word you're looking for, I think. You were afraid of being caught."

"You told me it was common knowledge that this sort of thing went on, and that you did the same thing—"

"That's true."

"And that your boss didn't lose a cent," Proust continued.

"That's false. Of course, I upped the prices. You were only waiting to be convinced."

Chamberland stood up and began to pace the room, speaking in the impersonal tone of voice he would use to dictate a letter.

"Then, later on, when Cavalier died, I had to draw pictures to show you how you could take his place." He stopped in front of the desk and asked coldly, "You remember that, too, I hope?"

But Proust was no longer looking at him. Instead he was fumbling nervously with a letter opener.

Chamberland continued, "I know you prefer not to relive those—how shall I put it—difficult moments, and that you tend to block them out of your memory. It's natural now that you've found your little niche. There's nothing like a comfortable armchair to cloud the memory! Unfortunately, I'm the wet blanket whose function it is to remind you that without me . . . . "

Chamberland walked over to the window and drew back the curtains.

"Look at this sunlit park, and all your fine horses. Without me, Proust, you'd be looking at something entirely different; you'd be rotting away, forgotten, in some prison."

"Don't be ridiculous! It wouldn't have gone that far."

"Do you want me to look it up in the criminal code for you? Breach of trust, forgery, embezzlement. . . . You'd have been lucky to get off with ten years."

"Only if Simone had noticed and prosecuted."

"And she would have if someone had let the cat out of the bag. But you had the clever idea of putting your trust in me. Thanks to my skill as an accountant, I not only corrected the situation, but turned it around in your favor, attributing all the losses to Cavalier's so-called mismanagement—"

"Since he wasn't around, it was no skin off his nose."

"Agreed. But on your own you'd have been incapable of such a sleight of hand. And it worked; you came out of it looking like the knight on the white horse, and three years later Simone succumbed to your attractions."

"I admit you helped me out of a tight spot, but look at what it's cost me. For the past ten years you've stuck to me like a bloodsucker! You take advantage of my love for Simone by threatening to reveal everything. Using our partnership as a pretext, you take almost all the company profits, and now you're prying the estate away from me."

"Don't talk so loud! I suppose you don't care whether your wife or mother-in-law hears us."

Proust jumped to his feet. His face was pale and his hands were trembling.

"It would probably be the best thing! Perhaps I should make a clean breast of it. Then I'd be free of you and I'll make sure I take you down with me!"

Like all weak men, Proust was subject to brief fits of anger. But it took more than that to affect Chamberland, who merely shook his head and looked on with amused sympathy.

"Don't be ridiculous. Our transactions have always been perfectly legal."

"I know. You're an expert at scientific blackmail!"

"What do you mean by blackmail? The fact that I ask for certain . . . compensations in return for services rendered? What do you expect me to do? I know human nature too well to hope for spontaneous gratitude. It's one of those feelings that always needs a little added incentive. Admit that once you married Simone, instead of giving me the thanks I deserved, you'd have been just as happy to toss me to the lions!"

"Of course not! Not if you'd been reasonable."

"What do you mean by that? That I should remain a family friend with the privilege of coming over from time to time on Sundays?"

"You're the lowest of the low."

"My dear friend, I'm only being reasonable. I have a heightened sense of justice, especially where I'm concerned. Without my intervention you would not be where you are today. I find it perfectly normal that you, and what you have, should belong to me."

Chamberland's tone was becoming increasingly biting. Proust was leaning against the wall. Even the way he held his body conveyed his weakness; with shoulders slumped and hands behind his back, he looked like a man about to be condemned. Yet his opponent's last words startled him into life.

"*Belong* to you?" he shouted. "Like a dog or a slave, I suppose. I still have enough pride—"

But the other man merely waved away his protestations.

"Forget about your pride. If everything goes well, you soon won't have to worry about it. The little summing up I just did applies to the past only. What concerns us is the future. Let's sit down and talk this over calmly."

He dropped into an armchair and lighted a cigarette, but the other man stood rooted to the ground.

"This is the beginning of a new era," continued Chamberland. "I hope that from now on we'll be able to consider ourselves true partners. There'll be no more talk of blackmail, and no more raking up the past. As a matter of fact, I'd like to forget our past relationship. What about you?"

"No. I know what your promises are worth."

"This time I'm serious. I'm smart enough to know that I've pulled the strings long enough and I shouldn't push my luck. What you said just now is fairly significant; you're at the point where you'd almost rather sink than swim. Is that it?"

"What does it matter?"

"It matters in that I've agreed to throw you a lifeline—as soon as your charming young stepdaughter asks me to, nicely. You must admit that my desire to marry Diana is an unhoped-for stroke of luck."

Proust shrugged. "If she accepts. Wanting to marry her is not enough."

"Do you think so? Experience has taught me that if you want something badly enough, you usually get it."

Proust's voice was bitter. "I wish you the best of luck."

"You could hardly do anything else. You have only two ways of getting me off your back, Proust: either you kill me—which would pose serious problems for you—or you become my father-in-law, which is rather humorous, you have to admit. In other words, you have no choice."

Chamberland stood up and looked in the mirror over the mantelpiece behind Proust. He smiled at his reflection. He said, smoothing his hair, "Romance is a luxury I haven't yet allowed myself. But if I'm going to be anybody's heartthrob, I'd better get started. I'm approaching forty and soon it'll be too late."

He looked at Proust, who was contemplating him with an indefinable expression in which servility mingled with contempt.

Chamberland laughed. "Of course there are practical reasons for my wanting to marry your step-daughter. Diana suits my tastes exactly. She's from an established upper-class family, with an impeccable background and all the social graces. I want to succeed in marriage the way I've succeeded in everything else. I want the best, in other words."

"You needn't bother explaining. I'm not interested in the way you feel."

Chamberland's pale cheeks flushed almost imperceptibly, but he continued to smile.

"I'm sorry. I simply wanted to convince you that I value Diana, and I hope that for *everyone's* interest she makes the right decision . . . and quickly."

FIVE MINUTES after Proust and Chamberland left the study, Paul went into the small living room adjoining the study and casually pressed the buzzer hidden behind the wall hanging.

This time it was Brigitte who noticed him through the French window as she returned with the children from their walk. She didn't beat about the bush.

"Are you looking for something, Paul?"

The young man offered her his most ingenuous smile.

"No, ma'am. I'm just checking something—I decided that I might as well find out what all this wiring is for." Then without transition, he added, "I've drawn the children's baths. Shall I take them upstairs?"

Brigitte made no further comment, but she was nonetheless intrigued.

Chapter 9

That evening Chamberland accepted the invitation to stay to dinner.

Aperitifs were served in the garden in the purple glow cast by huge umbrellas. Then, in the dining room, where the oak furniture glowed in the warm rays of the setting sun, a gourmet dinner was served. Finally cognac was offered in the twilight blue of the drawing room. Conversation died out when the sun slipped away, only to be revived when the lamps were turned on. It was an atmosphere of discreet elegance and luxury obviously enhanced by the distinction of past generations.

Only two members of the group knew the sordid details that lay behind this camaraderie, but not for an instant did they betray themselves as they strove to outdo each other with witty conversation and anecdotes. Chamberland made a point of humorously recounting his trip to show Diana that even in jet planes and palaces one encounters picturesque people and events. Proust, for his part, seemed eminently relaxed.

Brigitte was positively glowing with happiness. Only two hours earlier she had received a letter from her husband telling her that he would return to France in September. Only Mrs. Faber held herself apart from the general merriment and maintained her attitude of polite detachment. There was nothing unusual in this, however, for she always behaved this way in the company of Proust and Chamberland, neither of whom she liked.

Diana often felt Chamberland's eyes upon her, and did her utmost to turn away from his gaze. Time and again she told herself that this man loved her and that she must give his love a chance. She must look neither eager nor indifferent. But how tiresome it was to try to make her heart follow the dictates of her mind.

As he took his leave, Chamberland held her hand in his for a moment longer than necessary and asked in a low voice, "Will you walk me to my car?"

He had left it by the stables, which were a fair distance from the house. No doubt this was a calculated maneuver. As she walked along beside him, Diana cast about in vain for something to say, angry at the embarrassment that caused all thoughts to flee her mind. She was relieved when at last he broke the silence of the hot humid night.

"There are certain things I don't know quite how to express. I've always been inclined to look at other people's feelings without paying much attention to my own. It comes from being in business, from having to detect others' motives and predict their reactions. It's not unlike playing a game of chess and trying to foresee every move your opponent can make. The result of all this is that I'm incapable of coming to terms with myself."

Diana sensed that he had turned toward her and was searching out her eyes in the shadows.

"For the longest time I've fought against the image of you and what I feel for you." He fell silent and then asked, "But you already know all that, don't you?"

Diana nodded and then realizing that he couldn't see her, replied, "Mother has told me a great deal about you."

"I'm glad. I couldn't have hoped for anyone better to plead my case, since Simone and I are old friends and she's your mother. But I was afraid that you might find it old-fashioned of me to do such a thing."

"Why?"

"Well, in our grandmothers' day it was customary to confide in a girl's parents, so that she was often the last one in the family to find out she was loved."

"I'd never thought of it like that. Besides, I had an idea that . . . ."

She didn't dare finish the sentence. To tell him she had noticed he was interested in her might be interpreted to mean that without Simone's intervention the interest never would have been reciprocated. How complicated matters were becoming.

Chamberland, for his part, was equally cautious. He took no liberties whatsoever, not even that of slipping his arm under Diana's as it brushed against him. He went on in a humble tone of voice, "Thank you for not dismissing me lightly. You're so young, and I was afraid you wouldn't take me seriously."

"I don't find you old."

It occurred to Diana that such a banal answer was little better than ambiguous. She was afraid that Chamberland might read more into it than she intended.

"You barely know me, and I'm afraid you'll judge me harshly. Up until now, my name has always been associated with dry and none-too-pleasant financial matters. Do you think that you might be able to put that aside?"

Diana wondered whether he realized the significance of his question. In any case, she was grateful to him for having understood and expressed with such simplicity what constituted both the reason for their friendship, as well as the drawbacks. She could not help feeling that he deserved a frank reply in return.

"I don't know. I can only promise to try."

"I'll do my best to help you."

Then he added in a light tone, "I've decided to treat myself to a vacation. No more business trips, meetings or paperwork until I'm good and ready! And if you'd be so kind as to spend some of it with me . . . ."

Diana did not even think to reply, for they had reached the stables and her eye was caught by a long low form that stood out against the white walls. She went over to one of the doors and turned on the outside lights that lighted up the approach to the buildings.

"You've got a new car!"

"Didn't you tell me you found the other one a bit flashy?"

This one was anything but, although it still conveyed the impression of power and wealth. It was a midnight blue Mercedes as streamlined as an arrow. Chamberland began to laugh.

"Don't look so embarrassed. I've always been crazy about cars and I've wanted one of these for ages. It's always fun to get a new toy."

He examined his new acquisition with an air of detachment.

"Money imposes so many obligations on me that I deserve to indulge in a whim once in a while."

The word "obligations" reminded Diana of something Paul had said to her. "Wealth implies certain obligations." Unaware of what she was thinking, Chamberland continued his commentary.

"The problem is that poor people see only the whim being gratified without realizing what it truly costs."

These philosophical considerations were marred somewhat by the comment Chamberland tacked onto the end, a remark that was made unconsciously and betrayed his true nature.

"But, to get back to the car, I don't suppose I need to tell you that at the same time I concluded an excellent deal."

Diana made no reply, for she was worrying about how she would extricate herself from such a situation. But Chamberland merely asked, "Would you like to try it out tomorrow? I'll come and pick you up at about four; that'll leave you plenty of time to decide where you want to go."

He got into the car, and for what seemed an eternity, he held her hand in his through the open window.

He had the intelligence and self-restraint to drive off slowly, which impressed her much more than any demonstration of speed would have. She told herself it must require extraordinary strength of will to resist that temptation, given the power of the car and the fact that his only witness was a woman whose heart he hoped to win.

As she walked past the servants' quarters on her way back to the house, she noticed Paul leaning on his window sill, smoking a cigarette.

Her heartbeat quickened, although she could not quite say why. Probably he had seen her go off with Chamberland and was drawing his own conclusions. As if they meant anything to her! She wondered where he went when *he* left his room at midnight.

Thinking of this, Diana felt the absurd desire to seek revenge. Accordingly, as she passed below his window, she began to hum.

Chapter 10

A week later, Proust was convinced things were going well. As for Simone, she felt a renewed affection and gratitude toward her daughter. Diana, for her part, was able to play the game with ease and even conviction.

Every afternoon the midnight blue Mercedes would pass through the wrought-iron gate of the estate and glide silently along the long tree-shaded driveway. In the beginning, it would leave again almost immediately, but day after day it remained parked by the stables for increasingly longer periods of time. At first Diana had been enthusiastic about Chamberland's "new toy," but had soon grown to miss Prince and her rides in the forest.

One evening she alluded to this, only to have Chamberland turn up the next day in an impeccable riding outfit—highly polished boots, white ascot, olive-green jacket, and beige jodhpurs. Diana looked at him in open astonishment, an expression that could and did pass for admiration. In her eyes, he called to mind a store window, a catalog or a tailor's—anything but a horseback ride in the park. She couldn't help dropping a subtle hint to this effect.

"What a shame you're liable to get your outfit dirty!"

At the same time she realized with regret that her blue jeans were no longer suitable and that she'd have to put on formal riding gear, too. She duly complied, but not without feeling uncomfortable, especially when she ran into Paul at the foot of the stairs. And yet his face remained virtually impassive except that the ironic gleam in his eye seemed colder than usual.

Her embarrassment became even more acute when she met Chamberland in front of the stables. Julien, the stable boy who had just saddled the horses, gaped at her as if he couldn't believe his eyes. Diana felt the blood rush to her face, jumped onto her horse, and rode off straightaway, without even waiting for her companion who took a good minute to catch up.

"Well, I can see you're really in your element. The two of you look like something right out of a western. And you told me your horse was old," Chamberland said teasingly.

Diana replied, "He's just feeling his oats a little. Once he's had some exercise, he'll calm down."

"Lucky for me. I'm obviously not the equestrian you are."

He spoke the truth, but it was a superfluous confession, since Diana had already sized him up in a glance. He sat tensely in the saddle, anxiously watching his mount's ears as if they were some sort of indication of how it would behave. Diana was glad she'd had the sense to give him a gentle mare almost as old as Prince. Eventually her horse slowed to a walk and the ride progressed without incident.

But that day, and every other day, she made a detour so that she might avoid riding past Hazel Farm. She wondered just what Emilie would think if she saw her all rigged out. Diana had not been to visit her for quite some time and inexplicably, when she thought back to their last conversation, she felt ashamed. It was difficult to put her finger on the reason. It was as if Emilie had witnessed something—be it only an attitude toward life—that Diana was in the process of betraying.

But in fact she was not really betraying herself, but merely changing her point of view, or at least doing her utmost to do so. During the long rides that meant hours spent alone with Chamberland, she never stopped questioning herself and rationalizing her behavior.

When it comes down to it, I'm only doing what mother asked me to and following Brigitte's advice, Diana reasoned.

The thought of Brigitte was especially reassuring. Mrs. Faber, however, appeared to have removed herself from the situation. Never did she make any comment or ask any questions. Diana wondered whether she might be justified in interpreting this neutrality as approval.

At times Diana felt she was able to step aside and see herself riding along through the forest at the side of the man who had destroyed her trees and whom she had cursed only a few weeks earlier. At those moments she would look at him incredulously, as if only then discovering his presence. She would ask herself what piece of witchcraft caused him to be riding along beside her. And he, misunderstanding her expression, would smile, taking it for flattery.

Fortunately he was still as restrained as ever. Not once did he permit himself a tender word or gesture. His attitude remained one of friendly attentiveness. Only the questioning look in his eyes and the way he paused when speaking to create significant silences gave away his hopes and aspirations.

But even though Diana had to admit that he was a man of character, quality and wit, she could not bring herself to respond to him.

One evening she became especially aware of this.

They were approaching Templars' Crossing. Diana rode in silence, contemplating the vast bare spaces that held nothing save sun-scorched ferns curling up over the corpses of beech trees. The mossy earth was strewn with twigs and small branches. Piles of sawed-up timber on either side of the avenue stretched away as far as the eye could see.

Chamberland reined in his horse, examined the site, and then without looking at Diana said, "You hold this against me, don't you? All the trees that I've destroyed so that you hardly recognize the place."

This time he turned toward her to find that she was sitting motionless with a closed expression. He got off his horse and went over to one of the trees lying on the ground.

"Look at this," he said, pointing to the concentric

circles that grew darker near the center of the trunk.

Diana dismounted with an intrigued look on her face.

"These beeches look magnificent, don't they? They're as straight as a rod. But in reality they're completely rotten."

He pushed into the center of the trunk with his hand to demonstrate.

"They're just like sponge. I had to cut them down in the interest of the forest. A business doesn't have the right to be sentimental."

Diana remained silent, for she was surprised that he had read her mind and was furnishing an explanation that she had never asked for.

"Of course, I have the reforestation already planned. I've even ordered the new trees. The little Dianas who come after us will have an entirely new forest."

Diana couldn't help wondering whether he was alluding to starting a family. Almost everything he said seemed to contain a double meaning. In her embarrassment, she merely smiled. Chamberland interpreted this as a sign of encouragement and took her hand in his.

"I'm afraid you must see me as a usurper. The fact that I've acquired these woods that belonged to your family for more than a hundred years . . . ."

Diana was about to say, "You or anyone else!" but checked herself in the nick of time. Instead she replied, "My stepfather had to sell, didn't he? Now that I know you, it seems more like a minor misfortune."

Chamberland considered this comment for a moment with a smile of amusement. Seeing that Diana was worried about having made a faux pas, he went on to explain his amusement. "I can't quite figure out whether you've just given me a compliment or you're simply speaking your mind. In other words, should I interpret this 'minor misfortune' literally, or in a more figurative way?"

Diana understood that for the first time he was asking her a fundamental question, although it was well disguised. What he really wanted to know was whether she felt her family had lost the woods forever. Or, on the other hand, whether she was relieved that soon they might once again be part of the estate. Diana skillfully avoided the issue by countering with, "It's hard to say. I don't think I can quite cope with such linguistic subtleties!"

It was a reply that could pass for coquettishness. Chamberland seemed not to take offense, yet his expression grew sharper, proving that he was no dupe. Noticing this, Diana hastily glanced up at the sky and said, "I think we should head back. Those clouds look like they could bring a storm."

As she remounted, Diana was thinking to herself that she had managed to avoid the issue one more time, but that the second stage of her relationship with Chamberland—her second reprieve, in a sense—was quickly coming to an end. Everything served to remind her of her predicament. Even the avenue they were riding along was symbolic; one side of the forest had been destroyed, the other side was intact. They were riding along the border between two different domains and two different ways of life.

Diana fought against the tears that rose to her eyes, turning away to hide her face from Chamberland. Then, in a rush of confused emotion, she could see Paul with his laughing eyes and slender muscular body. But today, instead of distracting her from her problems, the thought of him inexplicably increased her perplexity, adding to it a sense of bitter remorse. No doubt he was not the least bit concerned about how she felt! Perhaps it was more regret than remorse—regret that every time they met she had given in to impulsive bursts of anger instead of . . . . Instead of what?

"You're thoughtful."

Chamberland was observing her with concern. Because his voice contained a subtle reproach, Diana did her best to smile.

"I'm sorry. It's just that I'm tired."

She was indeed tired, tired of playing her role and weighing every word she said. Chamberland, however, was content with this explanation.

"Now that I look at you, I can see that you're pale and you've got dark circles under your eyes. Let's go straight back to the house; I think you were right about the rain."

Once they reached the stables, he seemed to be waiting for an invitation that Diana couldn't bring herself to extend, so great was her desire to be alone. Finally he said, "Perhaps you should get some rest. I want you to look your best tomorrow night. I hope you haven't forgotten about the dinner party at my place. Even though most people are away on holiday, I found a few friends to invite."

No, Diana had not forgotten. During the past few

days the mere thought of spending the evening with people she didn't know and a man who remained a stranger to her had been enough to fill her with anguish.

As the Mercedes pulled away and the first drops of rain began to spatter on the driveway, Diana was seized by the desperate feeling of being caught in a trap from which she would never escape.

As she hurried through the now pouring rain toward the house, she remembered that once again no one except Melanie was home. Her parents had gone to Rouen after lunch, and Brigitte and her grandmother had taken the children to the seashore for a picnic. It was Paul's day off and no doubt he had taken his bicycle and gone off to one of his mysterious meetings.

Accordingly, Diana was surprised to hear the sound of a piano as she went in the front door. She stopped and stood stock-still, her heart racing and a lump in her throat, for the melody coming from the drawing room seemed to epitomize all the melancholy of the gray, stormy afternoon. She recognized Chopin's Prelude No. 15 as the music being interpreted with such poignant sensitivity.

As she tiptoed toward the sound, the notes of the music enveloped her in the desperate sweetness of contained passion. One note especially kept recurring, obstinately and obsessively, like a bell replying to the tinkling of raindrops on the veranda. Before even reaching the room, she knew with instinctive and absolute certainty that it was Paul.

Thinking the house empty, he was playing for himself.

The door was ajar, so she had only to peer around it. She could see him in profile in the blue green light streaming in the window. He was wearing a dark suit that she had never seen before. With closed eyelids and such an intent expression, he looked both younger and more serious than usual. Of his hands Diana could see nothing but their reflection in the polished wood of the piano, fluttering back and forth as if they were the very soul of the instrument.

That one note—like a drop of rain—continued to fall regularly. Outside the storm continued to growl, sending flashes of blue light through the windows.

Suddenly, as if inspired by the thunder and wind, the melody became low and solemn and then swelled to a feverish crescendo only to end with a heartrending cry.

Then came the silence that follows the awakening after a nightmare, and once more the music calmed and the note returned, the note that continued to fall and then died away. . . .

For a minute Paul sat motionless, staring off into the rain-drenched garden. Already the storm was moving off, and yellow light was coming in through the streaming windows. But the house was still buffeted by wet gusts of wind. A door slammed upstairs and the eaves sobbed their tears into the beds of flowers.

Diana then realized that all these sensations would be forever engraved on her memory; that instant during which nothing happened, during which time was suspended, was the culminating point in her life. She would ever after bear its mark. She would always be able to see herself standing in the doorway, held in the ineffable bittersweet confusion of emotion, watching a man who thought himself to be alone.

Paul's hands began to move over the keys again, but this time he was playing bizarre chords, improvising as he went along. He was still looking out the window, playing without any thought. And this syncopated dissonant music that expressed the confusion and perhaps even the suffering of his soul affected her even more profoundly than the Chopin had only a minute earlier. Even though she felt as if she were spying on him as he revealed one of his innermost secrets, she could not tear herself away.

Suddenly the piano was silent. Before she would draw away Paul had turned around and was staring at her. She watched him walk toward her. He did not smile, nor did he look embarrassed. He simply said in a solemn voice, "I'm sorry. I didn't think you'd be back so soon."

Diana's throat was dry; she was unable to utter a word so she shrugged slightly in reply to his apology.

"You're probably thinking that I'm taking advantage of things I have no right to. Music like this is a luxury, especially with such a magnificent piano," he said coolly.

Diana scarcely recognized him. His white shirt, elegant suit, and especially the hard look on his face and the hostile tone of voice that held not one bit of mockery all caused her to pale before him.

She was sure that for the first time he was playing no game and that he was revealing to her at that moment his very soul. She sensed that he was suffering, and far from being offended by his hostility she felt

she should take his hand and ask his pardon in turn.
But she merely stammered, "You play so . . . . I'm
sorry I interrupted you."

Paul seemed disconcerted and for several moments
studied the face raised toward his. Diana saw a
strange expression pass through his eyes, like a
shadow on frozen waters. She thought he might relax
and spare her, but the short silence gave him the time
to collect his thoughts and slip back into his role.

"Thank you for being so understanding. I did not
even hear the car leave. How fortunate that Mr.
Chamberland did not come back to the house with
you, as usual."

His tone and comments were ostensibly banal and
inoffensive. Yet Diana knew he was trying to hurt
her. She looked at him beseechingly. Why did he not
understand that something had changed that evening, that she was too tired to fight back and would
never again have the strength to take up the struggle?

But he went on cruelly, "I should have known
weather like this would have cut short your tête-à-
tête in the forest."

"Paul, please!"

"I see that I'm tiring you. I've noticed you haven't
been looking well lately. Most likely because of these
daily . . . ."

The irony was back in his voice, but his words
were loaded with hurtful allusions masked by
politeness. Diana knew she was defenseless. She was
neither indignant nor surprised. It was as if she had
expected this scene to take place and had resigned
herself in advance to his irony and criticism.

She murmured, not because she wished to fight back, but to prove that she understood what he was getting at, "You couldn't possibly understand."

He smiled an enigmatic smile.

"My role is not to understand but to serve."

Then he passed by her, coldly excusing himself, and walked off down the hallway. Diana listened to his footsteps as they faded away on the gravel outside. For a long time she remained where she was, leaning against the door, tears glistening on her eyelashes.

Chapter 11

Champagne, a haze of cigarette smoke, soft music and subdued lighting. Diana found herself drifting along in her own little universe; the laughing voices of the other guests seemed to reach her as if through a fog, and their faces were superimposed as if in a dream.

She could hear herself laughing and chatting, yet had the feeling that this was another young woman, one who had temporarily borrowed her gestures and voice. On the whole it was not the least bit unpleasant to feel removed from herself, as if she were a ship drifting along aimlessly wherever the current took her.

She was vaguely aware of having drunk too much, but could not quite remember how many times her champagne glass had been filled—four or five times or perhaps even ten. . . . It was the first time this had happened to her. The furniture and the floor seemed to rock back and forth whenever she stood up to walk around. Consequently, she remained seated as much as possible.

The only problem posed by sitting was that it was hard to stay put for more than ten seconds because the armchairs and sofas would begin to sway in the direction opposite that of the walls. The best solution of all was to dance, to abandon herself to a pair of arms that held her up and directed her, and to close her eyes so as not to see the swirling of silhouettes and objects.

From time to time her head would clear for a few fleeting moments. The mists would disappear, each face would again have a name, and inanimate objects would be reassuringly motionless. At such times she felt she actually knew where she was, for she would tell herself, *I'm at Chamberland's. . . . I'm dancing with Chamberland. . . . I'm only following Brigitte's and mother's advice. . . .*

But there was no way, in spite of any rationalizing, to escape the small gnawing feeling of guilt and remorse. It stubbornly remained no matter how many glasses of champagne she drank, or how many times she danced.

Diana finally admitted to herself that her feelings stemmed from regret and sorrow. And so that these moments might pass more easily, she decided to have another glass of champagne.

She walked over to the buffet with Chamberland at her side, conscious that he had not taken his eyes off her all evening. No longer did he hesitate to take her hand or put his arm around her waist. A few minutes earlier, while they were dancing, he had even tried to kiss her. Diana had responded with a peal of laughter, pretending to take his gesture for a joke, and implying that he, too, was slightly tipsy.

But in reality she could tell by the expression on his face and the tone of his voice that he was completely lucid. She knew that the party he had staged, with all its props and actors playing bit parts, was deadly serious business and that it marked the beginning of the third phase of their relationship. Chamberland had calculated every detail, leaving nothing to the whims of fate.

The romantic logistics of the relationship had been carefully planned. He had begun at a restaurant, on neutral ground; had then moved into the forest, Diana's domain; and finally ended up at his house, in his own territory.

The situation was rapidly growing more and more serious. Soon Diana would no longer be able to pretend she didn't understand. One day he would ask for her answer.

"Shall we dance?"

Soon Diana would have to commit herself not just for a dance, or an evening, but for the rest of her life. She stubbed out her cigarette, tossed back her hair, and sank into his arms. The music swept her away, scattering her thoughts to the wind. When the record stopped, she was barely aware that Chamberland continued to hold her close to him, his face a hair's breadth from her. Finally he released her regretfully, still caressing her with his eyes.

As time went on, Diana felt increasingly as if she were alone with him. The others were, of course, still there, but they no longer counted. Now they were, in her eyes, little better than shadows. She chatted and laughed with them, but forgot about them completely the moment they were out of sight. Chamberland alone remained part of reality.

He led her over to a French window opening onto the garden. Moths glowed briefly as they fluttered through the band of light streaming through the window. From the midst of the jumble of flowers came the night song of a toad. Diana felt a welcoming breeze on her damp forehead and closed eyelids.

Behind her the music had faded to a murmur, yet she could still hear the staccato chords of a piano. Images of the preceding day returned to obsess her: Prelude No. 15 blending with the symphony of the storm and Paul's rigid silhouette in the shadows of the drawing room.

Another more recent image joined these—that of herself several hours earlier walking down the stairs of her house to meet Chamberland, who was waiting for her outside. On the way she passed Paul who was going upstairs to draw the children's bath. He drew back to let her go by. His expression was distant and he refrained from uttering a word. Why, then, as she brushed past him, had Diana felt her knees weaken and her cheeks color, as a wave of sadness sent a chill through her heart?

Even tonight, surrounded by noise, and intoxicated by champagne and dancing, she was unable to forget him, unable to dismiss his silent reproaches and the suffering that his eyes held.

Diana felt she would have given almost anything

to be alone, in the silence of night, to be able to sort out this confusion of emotions.

But Chamberland was still there, with his hand on her bare arm, his breath on her cheek, and his soft yet strangely precise voice invading the private world of her thoughts and claiming her attention.

He was still doing his best to utter harmless comments in a casual voice. Yet underneath this feigned detachment, he was trembling with impatience, and Diana knew it.

"You haven't yet told me what you think of my latest acquisitions."

Chamberland was referring to a row of Norman cottages that were located not far from the estate. It went without saying that he had got a good deal on them.

Before dinner he had taken his guests on a tour of the property. They, of course, had marveled—and rightly so, Diana had grudgingly admitted—at his business acumen and good taste. Diana had already visited the site several times with her parents, but had never seen the completed project.

Seen from outside, surrounded by a garden of roses, the thatched-roof, cob-wall houses still retained their charming peasant-inspired qualities. But one had only to open any of the numerous hanging doors to realize that the interior had been completely remodeled and consisted of huge rooms often split into different levels. Where partitions had been removed, a few stairs connected the rooms. Highly polished copper and antique furniture stood out against stark white walls. In front of the tall stone chimneys were luxurious fur rugs. Green plants spilled out of black kettles. Oriental rugs covered the parquet floor. Chamberland had indeed outdone himself, and Diana and the others expressed their admiration.

Now he was saying, "I still have two houses to decorate. When I'm finished, you'll never know they were once used for livestock! For the moment I'm using them as storage rooms. Why, only today I took delivery of some magnificent Louis XV armchairs, signed by the craftsman."

Diana was hardly listening. The fresh air had cleared her head, but in spite of her good intentions she was incapable of working up any interest in her host's new possessions. She was simply thinking that Paul would probably appreciate them very much and that Chamberland should not be surprised if one day he found the young man ensconced in one of his period chairs.

"But what you said only a short while ago is my greatest reward."

Just what had she said? Probably that she loved the buildings, as everyone else had.

"Because I bought those houses with you in mind and I had them remodeled for you, thinking that one day . . . ."

She smiled and passed her hand over her forehead to imply that she didn't feel well and that he had chosen the wrong time to venture into a conversation of that nature. But instead he chose to think she was confused or embarrassed and tried to press his advantage.

"I love you, Diana. This is the first time I've had the courage to come right out and tell you so. You're so young and beautiful. More than anything else in the world I want you to accept the life I can offer you."

Diana knew that the declaration was inevitable. Luckily Chamberland asked no direct questions. He was even tactful enough to make it clear that he didn't yet expect any definite reply.

"I'm not asking you to make any decision. I simply want you to think things over, knowing that I'll do everything in my power to see that you're happy. I'm no longer a boy. I've reached the age when reason reinforces and guarantees one's feelings. Because of that, I'm absolutely sure—"

The noise of an approaching car cut him off. As a beam of light swept across the garden, every detail of the landscape seemed to spring out of the shadows. Chamberland went forward a step or two, his eyes betraying his surprise.

"Who could it be at this hour?" Diana asked.

"Let's go see," he muttered.

Diana complied and followed along, with the premonition that this late arrival had something to do with her. But she was not at all prepared for the shock she was to receive.

A man stepped out of the shadows into the light coming through the window and bowed ceremoniously. A cry of joy escaped Diana's lips.

"Paul!"

Instinctively she pulled her arm away from Chamberland and moved apart from him. Chamberland contemplated the intruder with a scowl.

"I've seen you at the Prousts', haven't I? Aren't you one of their servants?"

Paul bowed again, this time as stiffly as an automaton.

"I work for Mrs. Robin, Mrs. Proust's sister."

"What do you want?"

"Miss Diana."

"What?"

"Please excuse me. What I mean is that I was told to come and pick her up."

"And who gave you this order?"

"Mrs. Faber, who is Mrs. Proust's mother, and consequently—"

"I know. But why?"

"You will excuse me, sir, I hope, for not being able to answer that question. My role is to carry out orders, not to question them."

Diana could hardly repress the desire to guffaw, but she managed to ask with simulated concern, "I hope grandmother isn't sick?"

"I think not, but I couldn't say for sure—"

Chamberland interrupted again, in tones of arrogant irritation. "Mrs. Faber had no need to give you a complete explanation. I assume, however, that you have some idea of the reason she sent you."

"I should like to point out, with all due respect, that my position allows me no opinions."

"Quit playing the clown, will you?"

"Since you do me the honor of asking my opinion and since my position does allow me to conjecture, I suggest that out of worry—which is nothing surprising on the part of a grandmother—and given her granddaughter's extreme youth and the obvious signs of fatigue she has lately shown, Mrs. Faber perhaps decided that too much socializing after a certain hour, even in the best of company, might have unfavorable effects on the young lady's health. Of course, I might also mention the older generation's keen sense of decorum, which leads them to fear all sorts of dangers, both real and imagined, which—"

"Are you trying to make a fool of me?"

Cut off in midsentence, just as he was really getting into stride, Paul assumed a foolish and vaguely indignant expression.

"How could you ever . . . ?"

Chamberland glared at him in haughty anger. Diana stared at the toes of her shoes, not daring to look up, for fear of laughing out loud. For all of a sudden—was it because of the champagne—she felt inexplicably relaxed and lighthearted. It seemed to her for the first time that she could make sense of the evening.

"What do you think?" Chamberland had turned toward her, forgetting to adjust his brusque tone of voice. "This is absurd, to say the least!"

"Yes, I don't quite see . . . ." Diana's voice trailed off, for if the truth be known, she was not especially intrigued by Paul's appearance or the reasons for it. For her, the most important thing was to have rediscovered the old Paul with his barely perceptible irony and unexpected drollness hiding under a veneer of impeccable politeness. Yesterday's Paul, the stranger whose every word and expression were hurtful, faded into the past.

For all his shrewdness, Chamberland was obviously light years away from understanding the workings of Diana's mind. He must have taken her absentminded air for confusion because he went on to say, "But I'd always thought your grandmother was so open-minded and up-to-date."

This time it was Diana's turn to frown, deeming it inappropriate for him to make such a comment. Chamberland turned back to speak to Paul.

"Tell Mrs. Faber— No, perhaps I'll telephone her myself. You may go."

But the young man didn't budge.

"As you wish. But allow me to point out that it is after midnight and that everyone will be sleeping. Not to mention that you may encounter some difficulty having the call put through, since the village operator tends to sleep like a log while on duty—"

"Keep your advice to yourself! I'll do as I please! Good night!"

Paul bowed slightly, but still did not move an inch.

"In that case, Miss Cavalier will no doubt—"

"I'll see her home myself in a few minutes. You've made your point—Mrs. Faber is probably sleeping. Why don't you go do the same thing and leave us alone!"

But Diana thought she saw a worried look in Paul's eyes and so ventured to say, "Don't you think it would be better . . . ?"

Chamberland forced a smile.

"But, darling, you can't just rush off like that and leave our guests. They're probably wondering where we are right now. If anyone gets upset about when you get home, I'll take the blame."

With that he took Diana's arm and with a no-nonsense attitude led her back into the living room. She sensed Paul was walking away, but didn't dare turn around. Her thoughts were so jumbled that she didn't know what to make of them. Her grandmother had always been so cautious and reserved that it was inconceivable she would step in. She had said nothing about a curfew during the day. Moreover, it was strange that she should have asked Paul to pick her up. Diana could only conclude that his story was decidedly suspicious.

But it was impossible to linger in thought once she was caught up again in the whirl of the party. Chamberland led her over the buffet and poured her a glass of champagne, which she sipped halfheartedly. Soon she felt as if she had dreamed the scene that had just taken place outside.

She began to dance, this time to a slow, almost soporific rhythm. Perhaps it was because of the stuffy atmosphere after the refreshing coolness of the garden that she felt slightly dizzy. In any case, her heart was heavy with a sense of regret she could not quite define.

She no longer had even the strength to smile. As she looked up, she caught a glimpse of herself in the mirror—pale skin, wide eyes and set features. She felt as she had earlier, as if she were looking at a stranger whom she slightly pitied. Chamberland murmured something in her ear, but the words did not sink in right away.

"I'm sorry we were interrupted by that fool. I really can't understand . . . ."

Diana, however, had no desire to understand. She

could only repeat to herself that Paul had come to get her and wanted to take her away and that she had not gone with him because she couldn't.

These thoughts, which turned slowly in her mind to the same rhythm as the music, both reassured and worried her.

"I'd love a little more champagne! I'm dying of thirst!" she said, trying to change the topic.

The blue clouds of smoke had dried her lips and throat, leaving her parched. Besides, she felt there was something she had to drown in the bubbling liquid, although she was not quite sure what it was, and idly dismissed the thoughts.

As the cool bubbles tickled her nose she laughed in earnest at Chamberland, for he was extraordinary. He looked as fresh as ever. His ascot was impeccable and his skin flawless. There was not even a drop of perspiration on his forehead.

She was still laughing when he took her in his arms on the dance floor. But then he led her to the far end of the living room and into another room lighted by a single lamp with a dark blue shade.

She saw his face close to hers and then felt his lips kissing her forehead and eyelids. She felt as if she were more a prisoner of her own weakness than of his strength; if he were to leave her at that moment she might not be sure enough on her feet to make her way back alone without stumbling.

Fortunately Chamberland retained all his self-control. He was neither nervous, nor carried away by emotion; his feelings remained in check and his voice perfectly calm.

"Diana, darling, forgive me. Please don't judge

me. Tonight I feel as if another part of me has taken over. I've met difficult opposition many times in my life, and I've always defeated my opponents. But for the first time I feel as if I'm at someone else's mercy."

Diana stared at him, eyes wide. Later on she would recall these words, but as yet they had not registered. Her expression was grateful rather than hostile, for she realized that Chamberland might have taken advantage of her weakness to obtain exactly what he wanted without meeting much resistance on her part.

"May I kiss you, really kiss you?"

She smiled to play for time as she searched for some way to refuse without hurting his feelings. Then suddenly he stiffened. Diana saw him raise his head and listen attentively, as if something out of the ordinary had taken place.

The music coming from the living room had stopped. The women's laughter was transformed into cries of fear. Men's voices were heard above the din, as well as strange fragments of sentences.

"Telephone the fire department. . . . It may be too late. . . . There's someone . . . . Everyone stay calm! Chamberland . . . where's Chamberland?"

Chamberland hurried toward the door, only to bump into one of his guests. Diana recognized the doctor.

"What's going on?"

"Something is burning in one of your houses. The one at the far end."

"Burning? Impossible! How do you—"

"Come and see for yourself! Luckily there was a garden hose. I don't think it'll spread."

Unsteadily, Diana followed the men. There was no

one around to notice that she was none too sure on her feet. It was a relief to be able to breathe the cool night air once more.

A strange gathering came into focus before her eyes. Car headlights had been turned on and shadows were moving about in the horizontal beams of light. To one side was a light-colored mass that turned out to be a group of women in pastel evening clothes. Beyond, she could make out a waving snakelike hose projecting a stream of water that met the flames inside the house with a resounding crackle.

She drew closer, eyes riveted to the silhouette holding the stream of water, and recognized Paul.

Abruptly Chamberland's furious voice was heard above the din.

"My armchairs! They'll be ruined! Stop that, damn you! Can't you see, the fire's out!"

But Paul went even closer to the window, as if taking Chamberland's words for encouragement, and made sure that the inside of the house was thoroughly doused. The sound of crackling wood filled the air.

Chamberland sprang forward to snatch the hose from him, only to receive its full force directly in his face. Suddenly the drama was transformed into slapstick comedy. Paul refused to release his hold, and the stream of water shot to one side, coming to rest on the crowd of onlookers. The group of pastel dresses rapidly dispersed amid loud protestations.

"Stop, you idiot!" Chamberland cried.

"If you would be so kind as to let go . . . ."

The two men had the stage to themselves since the doctor, barrister, industrialist, future cabinet minister and the others had all retreated, dripping, behind parked cars. From out of the darkness came various orders.

"Let him go, will you?"

"He's right! You're the one who's soaking us!"

Pale with humiliation and rage, Chamberland finally gave in. Paul placed the hose on the ground and went to turn off the tap. Calm reigned once again as the assorted guests came out of hiding to mop themselves off. A voice sang out, "He's done it . . . the fire's out!"

And then another took up the commentary. "There's no chance of it catching again; it's a regular swimming pool in there."

Chamberland had by this time recovered all his former haughtiness.

"Are you mad? What possessed you?"

"To put out the fire? I'm not quite sure myself. . . ."

Paul, as usual, was completely at ease, in spite of the fact that every pair of eyes was trained on him.

"Am I to understand that you don't approve of my taking this initiative?" he continued.

"And just how did the fire start?" Chamberland's voice was harsh.

"I regret I cannot clear up that point."

"Are you quite sure?"

"Just now, after being dismissed by you, I was on my way back to my car—or rather the one lent to me by Mrs. Robin, when I thought I smelled something burning. I went over to the house, and although I didn't actually see any flames, there was a reddish glow. Accordingly, instead of wasting time by sounding the alarm, I thought it best to take steps—"

"And what was the cause of this glow?"

"Why the fire, of course. Look for yourself. It was a Louis XV armchair, a very beautiful one, as far as I could see—"

"And it burst into flames, just like that, in the middle of the night?"

At this point a third party intervened. It was the barrister, who asked of Chamberland, "Do you know this man?"

"Vaguely. He works for Proust."

"Was his presence here justified?"

"He came to pick up Diana."

"Do you have specific reasons to suspect him?"

"Not exactly, but since—"

"A word to the wise, old man. You're accusing a man who may well have done you a big favor. If you think this is an act of mischief, then lodge a complaint, but don't make accusations, without proof, in front of witnesses."

Chamberland demonstrated his self-control by responding with a good-natured smile.

"You're right. I'm spoiling everyone's evening. We can clear this up some other time. Let's get back to the party."

And then he said to Paul, "As for you, if you've nothing to do with this, you'll have your reward. In the meantime, why don't you stay for a drink? My maid will get you something."

"I am most grateful, but if you don't mind, I think

I'd rather carry out my orders and drive Miss Cavalier home."

Chamberland barely contained another outburst of anger.

"You're persistent, aren't you? I told you I'd take care of that myself."

No one saw exactly what happened next, not even Diana, who was anxiously watching their every move. Some of the men went to turn off their headlights, while a group began to make their way back to the living room. Chamberland had just turned his back on Paul, who responded by taking his arm and seemingly said something in hushed tones.

Both men stopped dead. Diana thought she saw Chamberland's features betray complete astonishment. For several seconds he gaped at Paul and then conceded, "Very well. As you wish!"

Chamberland went over to Diana, hesitated slightly, and said, "You seem tired, darling, and after all . . . . I'm afraid the party will go on longer than I'd planned. You understand; I have to try to help my guests forget about this little incident. Perhaps you should take advantage of the opportunity. . . ."

The entire evening had been one puzzle after another. But Diana was in no state to analyze the cause of this complete reversal of opinion, let alone even wonder about it. She was unable to think beyond the immediate; she would be able to leave with Paul and at the same time escape Chamberland's declarations of love, as well as the tiresome chore of bidding the other guests good-night.

Moreover, no one gave her even a moment to consider the matter or say goodbye hastily. An energetic hand took her by the arm and almost marched her off to the car. An abrupt start threw her back against the seat. Wall, trees and bushes rushed past with dizzying speed.

Diana protested weakly, "Please, not so fast! My head is spinning."

"Good! I hope it comes completely unscrewed!"

This was indeed Paul's voice, but it was entirely devoid of the respect he usually showed her. Diana wanted to point this out to him, but couldn't quite find the words. And in any case, she most likely wouldn't have the courage to speak them aloud.

Nonetheless Paul had slowed down and opened his window to let in fresh air. He was observing his passenger out of the corner of his eye. Diana tried to look at him sternly, but couldn't quite manage it.

She wanted him to stop the car so that she could get out and walk. But she refrained from asking, because to do so would be to admit that she had drunk too much, and invite Paul to continue to browbeat her. This night, above all others, was the one when she was most in need of sympathy and gentleness. But he had no way of knowing just how unhappy she really was.

"There are times when I wish I were dead!"

Diana managed to utter this comment without any melodramatic overtones and in a voice so low that she might have been talking to herself.

Paul, however, merely commented dryly, "You get depressed when you drink. Maybe you'll keep that in mind next time."

And as if this proof of callousness weren't enough, he added sternly, "At times like this, one's true nature often comes through."

Diana, however, was not quite thinking clearly enough to reply.

"And as for Chamberland," Paul continued bitingly, "wine tends to mellow him, don't you think? But that's exactly what I expected. Maybe you're depressed because you had to leave him so suddenly."

This time Diana made a superhuman effort to grasp the implication and finally met with success.

"Be quiet! You have no right . . ." she stammered.

"No right to do what?"

"To say . . . to think such things. . . ."

"Forgive me. I assumed it was almost official, since just now I heard him coaxing you and calling you 'darling.' Naturally I concluded—"

"There's nothing to conclude! I . . . I feel so dizzy! Could you stop the car for a minute?"

Her small pathetic voice struck a responsive chord in Paul's heart. He braked gently, stopped the car, and turned off the headlights. They found themselves surrounded by the lively freshness of the night air filled with the rustling of leaves and the hoot of owls.

"I'd like to walk a little," Diana murmured.

"Do you think you can?"

He hurried around to the other side to help her out. Diana clung to his arm.

"My shoes hurt," she explained.

"I see."

"You don't believe me, do you?"

With two swift kicks she sent them spinning into the middle of the road, reducing her height by two or three inches. Paul, who suddenly found himself that much taller, stood motionless.

"Put them back on, right now!"

"No! I want to walk barefoot in the grass. I can if I want! You have no right . . . ."

"Put your shoes back on, and then I'll give you my jacket."

"Your jacket? Why? I'm roasting."

"Your dress is all wet, and you're shivering. I don't want you to catch pneumonia."

"I can if I want. At least if I did, you'd be nicer to me."

In the moonlight Paul stood out as a vague yet foreboding symbol of rectitude. Diana's frail silhouette clung to him as if she were a castaway hanging onto a reef for dear life.

"Listen to me, little one. If you don't do as I say in the next ten seconds I'll let you walk back to the house by yourself."

Diana stared at him hesitantly.

"You'd never do that! I'd be so frightened. . . ."

Nonetheless, one after the other, her feet found her shoes, which slipped and slid on the pavement as she tried to step into them. Paul came to her aid and then took off his jacket and placed it around her bare, slender shoulders.

"All right," said Diana seriously. "I accept, but only because I'm cold and because you called me 'little one.' I always agree when I'm asked nicely."

"Unfortunate, but true."

"Why do you say that?"

"No reason. I don't think you're in any state to understand."

"But there's not much to understand! Suppose you said to me, 'Diana, little one, I'm dying to kiss you—"

"Don't worry, I wouldn't say that."

"Why not? There you go again, being nasty. You never believe anything I say. But it's true that *I'm* dying to kiss *you*. . . ."

"Be quiet. You don't know what you're saying."

"Of course, I do. I'm feeling much better since I got out of the car."

"In any case, you've found your tongue."

"I've wanted to kiss you again for the longest time. In fact, since the day I found you in my little house."

"You could have fooled me."

"I remember it perfectly. You had a sunburn on your nose, and one of the buttons on your shirt had come off. I'd have sewn it back on, but we got sidetracked, didn't we?"

"Diana—"

"And then when you spoke to me yesterday in the drawing room, you hurt me so much. And I cried because of it—"

"You cried?"

"Yes. But it doesn't make any difference to you."

Paul stopped suddenly and drew the two lapels of his jacket closer together, thus imprisoning Diana. He scrutinized the pale finely featured face turned toward his, and then said in a low shaking voice, "I don't know whether you realize . . . whether you understand . . . what you just said—"

"What did I say now? You still look angry."

"Just as I thought. You don't even remember."

"Tell me just what you mean by these . . . these insinuations. Is it because I drank a few miserable glasses of champagne? In the first place, I only drank them because of you."

"Me?"

"Yes. Because I've been depressed ever since . . . ever since you made me cry. So there!"

"Diana, little one, listen to me and pay attention. Is it true . . . do you really think of me from time to time?"

"No. Not from time to time. All the time. And it complicates everything. If I weren't so tired, I'd explain it to you."

"You don't have to. I understand."

Diana saw a smile begin to play about his lips. She shook her head in exasperation. "No! You don't understand anything. And the proof is that I'm upset, and all you do is make fun of me."

"No. I was smiling because you're tired and right now all these words aren't terribly important."

"Of course they are. They're extremely important!"

"No. We're in the middle of the countryside, in the middle of the night on some secluded little-known road. We've escaped from time and space, and life itself. All I can see of your face is your light skin and the dark spots that are your eyes and mouth. And, my little one, I in turn can tell you something very tender and very secret because we have left memories behind and tomorrow you will have forgotten. I love you. . . . I've loved you since the first moment I laid eyes on you, when I saw your reflection among the water lilies in the pond."

Diana closed her eyes so that she might drink in these words that, unbeknownst to her, she had waited so long to hear. Paul's voice was like a warm gentle caress, without a trace of irony or bitterness.

"At first I loved only your reflection, a fairy tale that rippled with the wind on the water. A maiden with golden hair on a white palfrey. And then one Sunday, with the ringing of the church bells and the buzzing of the cicadas, in a tiny thatched house whose windows were covered with ivy, you took on a face and body. And I came to love them, too, just as passionately and desperately."

The last word made Diana shiver as she repeated it involuntarily.

"Desperately?"

"Well, let's just say I had no hope. Because, if I deliberately flaunt some regulations—remember the No Trespassing signs—I realize that certain things are out of bounds. . . . And so, on my image of you and my love for you I put a little sign: Happiness and Love Not Allowed."

"But why? What you said just awhile ago was so beautiful, and now . . . now, I'm all confused again!"

"It doesn't matter. When you awake tomorrow you'll have forgotten all this. Let's go."

"No! I want to stay with you, Paul. I don't want to forget anything."

"Come, my dearest love. I want to remember this moment forever. It's a fragment of eternity that will belong to us always, that we must preserve at all costs. But we must also have the courage to take up life again where we momentarily left it."

Yet Paul made no move. Their eyes remained locked together. Seconds passed, diaphanous and fragile, casting a magical spell that even the slightest gesture might break.

Finally Diana whispered, "Paul, kiss me, kiss me as if there were no tomorrow!"

It was the only way to shut out the words that caused pain. She freed one of her arms and slipped it around his neck. It was the only way to be sure that his face bathed in shadows actually did exist, and to draw it close to hers.

And suddenly, with stars in her eyes, she felt a profound almost dizzying feeling of tenderness take hold of her and banish her pain. . . .

Paul's jacket slid slowly from her shoulders and fell noislessly to the ground.

Chapter 12

When Diana awoke next morning she expected a king-sized hangover.

But after only a few hours of sleep, she found herself astonishingly alert, her mind clear and her body refreshed. She jumped out of bed and bounded over to the window to draw back the curtains and welcome a day that she found very nearly as heady as champagne itself. Instead of the drawn features and haggard eyes that are normally the result of intemperance, the bathroom mirror presented her with a pair of luminous eyes and a rosy complexion.

A mysterious feeling of joy had taken hold of her very being and penetrated every fiber of her body. Her mind was functioning in a state that could only be described as lucid intoxication. Seen from this perspective, the cares of the preceding day seemed little more than trifling details. In vain did she try to remember how, for even a moment, she had considered marrying a man for pragmatic reasons—a man she didn't love and never would. The old conflict between heart and mind no longer applied. There was no longer any conflict, since the heart was always right.

In the shower Diana felt like singing these thoughts at the top of her lungs as the cold water washed away all her qualms and doubts. Her fortune, her forest, her house—all of them could go to the devil if her very happiness was the price she had to pay to keep them.

Happiness. Diana felt as if she were uttering the word for the very first time. Up until then, happiness had represented something vague that one hoped for without really being able to define. How easy it had once seemed to renounce this abstract notion, to willingly make a vague promise to exchange one's life for material possessions.

But last night happiness had suddenly taken on shape and sense in the most dazzling way possible, and had acquired infinite value.

In spite of Paul's prediction that she would have forgotten everything on awakening, Diana remembered even the most minute details of their conversation in the middle of the countryside. Every word they had uttered was engraved in her memory. She could still feel his arm around her shoulders, feel the weight of his face as it brushed against hers.

Out of that kiss had sprung knowledge that had lain dormant within her since the first time he had kissed her—she was in love with Paul.

Nothing else mattered.

Diana put on her prettiest summer dress. It was the least she could do to show fate that she appreciated the favors bestowed on her and prove to Paul that it was possible to drink too much champagne and still wake up the next morning feeling wonderful.

Diana went off to seek him out, trembling with impatience at the thought of their being face to face once more. She wondered how he would react. She could picture him with eyes darkened by a night of insomnia, looking at her in surprise and confusion and whispering her name. Then again he might simply take her in his arms without saying a word to express his fervent emotion. Unless he waited in thoughtful silence until she took the first step.

Naturally, none of these hypotheses conformed to reality. Paul was in the laundry room, busy doing the washing. The setting was obviously not conducive to a love scene.

Paul was neither surprised nor confused when she appeared in the doorway.

"Hello!" he called out in a voice that held not one iota of tenderness. "How nice of you to come and visit me. You arrived in the nick of time; I was beginning to get discouraged. I've always hated this sort of thing."

He walked toward her, wiping his hands on his blue apron as he commented, "Whew, it's hot in here. And to think that people actually pay to get into steam baths!"

He looked Diana over critically.

"Congratulations! You look more beautiful and elegant than ever. Champagne must be good for you.

It's heightened your color, the way dew makes flowers even more vibrant. But don't look so upset. Dirty laundry always brings out the poet in me."

He was adopting exactly the same attitude as during their first meetings. Luckily he hadn't gone back to calling her Miss Cavalier! Diana stepped forward.

"Paul, please don't start that again."

"Start what?"

"Joking and making fun of me. I don't feel like laughing or getting angry."

"Then what's left? Now you've gone and complicated matters." There was an underlying ring of coldness to his tone.

"Is that . . . is that all you have to say to me?" she stammered.

Paul shrugged. "I'm afraid you've lost me."

Diana tried desperately to find some correlation between the preceding night and the present. On the one hand, Paul had taken her in his arms and whispered words of love. On the other he was now more distant than ever, as if he was doing his best to destroy the memory of that night. Diana said in a sorrowful tone of voice, "I didn't expect such . . . such coldness."

"I'm sorry if I seem cold to you. You're imagining things. Perhaps you do feel under the weather today."

Diana turned away with tears stinging her eyes. No matter what it cost her, she must not let Paul see them. From now on pride would be her only refuge. This time he had cut her to the quick. She stiffened and said as casually as she could, "I'm touched by your concern, but I don't understand it. Anyway, it's not important. From now on I won't try to understand. Goodbye."

She was sincere in what she said. At that moment she had only one desire—never to see or hear him again.

But just as she turned to leave he reached out and grabbed her arm.

"No. That would be a mistake! Listen to me. . . ."

Diana tried to free herself, but he drew her back into the steamy room.

"Listen to me. I'm acting like a coward and I know it. I should let you go. I promised myself I would, but . . . I just don't have the courage."

"The courage to do what?"

"To let you go thinking the worst of me."

"But that's exactly what you deserve."

"I know. I'm a bundle of contradictions. A minute ago I'd have given anything to make you go away. But now I want you to stay."

"For what? So that you can make fun of me?"

"Oh, my darling, don't you see, it's a defense reflex."

"Against me?"

"Against my feelings and my weakness. While I'm cracking my stupid jokes, I can forget how I feel about you."

"But last night—"

"Last night was the exception that proves the rule. Last night we were two anonymous shadows with neither a past nor a future. Today we're back where we belong. Here I am with my dirty laundry—"

"But I came to tell you—"

"Don't say a thing, Diana. It'll only make things harder. I'm older and wiser than you. Your sweetness and sincerity are no match for the obstacles separating us."

"What obstacles?"

"Real ones, concrete ones: land, forest, houses—"

"But you told me they weren't important to you."

"They aren't but they're part of your world. They form an insurmountable barrier between us. I can move into your little house, but I can't move into your life," Paul finished gently.

"Oh, Paul no, no. That's only your pride speaking."

"Pride and a sense of caution. If I broke certain regulations your family would disown you, little one. You'll always be a prisoner of what you own; you're caught in a golden trap and I'll never be able to set you free."

Diana felt a hopeless sense of desperation flood her.

"But I may find myself freed by circumstances. Unless I marry Chamberland, I'll be as poor as you. I've already been fully briefed on the matter."

"I know and I can't bear the thought." Paul came a step closer. Suddenly his expression was hard and pained. "I can't stand the thought of you and Chamberland . . . ."

"Chamberland and me?"

"Last night when he put his arm around you and called you 'darling' I almost killed him!"

"Poor Chamberland! He had a narrow escape!"

"He certainly did. Instead, I set one of his chairs on fire, but if he hadn't given in—"

"*You* did that?"

"Who else? And all those hours you spent alone in the forest with him. All those flourishes and platitudes he spouted in his sugary voice. And you ate it all up like the silly little goose that you are."

"Why, thank you!"

"Don't you realize what people will think? Don't you realize how you've behaved? Why, he's twenty years older than you."

"It's wonderful!"

"What is? That he's twenty years older?"

"What you just said. It proves that anything is possible. You love me, Paul! You love me and you're jealous!"

Paul took another step forward and said threateningly, "Don't talk nonsense. Yes, I love you. I haven't changed since last night. It's ridiculous, but what can I do? But I'm not jealous."

"Then I don't quite understand what you have against Chamberland."

"I can't stand the sight of him."

"And why did you come and get me? I mean, take me away."

"Because I didn't think those people were right for you."

"I thought you were following grandmother's orders."

"I . . . . Exactly! Your grandmother didn't approve of that party."

"Did she actually tell you that?"

"I could see it in her eyes."

A strange silence came over them. Paul still looked furious, but at the same time a sort of confusion bordering on anguish spread over his face. Diana smiled without taking her eyes off him. Then she stepped forward, and leaned her head against his chest.

"You scared me so with your coldness just now. I thought everything was over."

"But it has to be over."

"No, Paul. It can't be."

"We never even should have begun."

"Don't say that. Don't say or think anything. Just hold me close, the way you did last night. Because I love you, too, and nothing else matters. It would be so stupid not to take the happiness that's offered to us."

This time Paul seemed to accept defeat. He bent his head, brushing Diana's hair with his lips, and echoed, "Happiness . . . . A little girl who thinks love equals happiness. My dearest little one, full of innocence. But I predict that we'll come up against—"

At that moment Paul sensed a shadow blocking the light coming through the door. Raising his eyes, he saw Simone Proust, pale and tight-lipped, watching them from the hallway.

She stared at him for a moment, but Paul didn't flinch. Then she walked away without saying a word. Diana suspected nothing. Paul held her more tightly.

"All sorts of complications," he finished with a sigh.

Chapter 13

Paul's prophecy turned out to be true. The complications he spoke of began the very same day, shortly after lunch.

Simone burst into the hall just as Paul was coming out of the drawing room carrying a large opaline vase. Both stopped dead and stared at each other in stormy silence. Then Simone launched an all-out attack.

"How dare you even set foot in this house!"

The young man made a stiff little bow.

"I came to get this so that I could wash it," he said casually. "You may have noticed that I took upon myself the task of cleaning all the vases in the house. And now, if you'll excuse me, I must wash Mrs. Robin's car—"

"No need! You no longer work for my sister!"

Paul smiled ingenuously.

"I don't quite understand."

"Really? Must I draw pictures? You're fired! Is that clear enough?"

"Perfectly."

"I suppose you know why?"

"In other words—"

"In any case, I don't owe you any explanation. Just keep in mind that I never want to see you in this house again."

"I wonder what Mrs. Robin will have to say about this?"

An angry flush rose to cover Simone's neck and cheeks. "How dare you! How dare you be so rude to me! Get out! I don't want to look at you a minute longer!"

Paul frowned and put on his most dignified expression.

"Am I to understand that as of this minute I am no longer employed here?"

"Yes! You're fired! Are you a complete imbecile?"

Paul said, with feathers completely unruffled, "It's a pity about this vase. A minute ago it was safe and sound. Strange how the fate of inanimate objects, as well as that of humans, can hang on such a slender thread."

With that he opened his arms and the opaline vase shattered into a hundred fragments on the marble floor.

"There! My work is done."

Horrified, Simone leaned against the wall and gazed in dismay at the fragments on the floor.

At that very moment Brigitte dashed into the hall.

"What happened?" she asked searching their faces. "What broke?"

"The large Empire vase from the drawing room," supplied Paul.

"But how?"

"If you would care to ask Mrs. Proust . . . ."

These few comments enabled Simone to recover.

"I can explain, Brigitte. But right now, kick him out of the house, I beg of you!"

"But why? Because he broke the vase? It's a shame, but things like this happen to everyone. It's no reason to—"

Simone began to wring her hands.

"It's not that," she groaned.

Paul untied his blue apron. For Brigitte's benefit he explained, "You have mistaken a consequence for a cause, Mrs. Robin. In other words, I wasn't fired because I broke the vase, I broke the vase because I was fired."

Briggitte's eyes grew wide as saucers. "I don't understand any of this!"

Paul handed her his apron. "If you would be so kind as to take this symbol . . . ."

"Is this some kind of a joke?"

Simone sprang to her sister's side, grabbed her arm, and almost shouted, "No, Brigitte, no! It's not a joke! Please, trust me . . . get rid of him. And tell Diana I must see her in the study right away. We might as well get this over with. I'm going to take some aspirin."

"Here you are." Paul held out a small metal tube. "I'd advise you to dissolve them in a half a glass of sugared water—"

In answer Simone turned on her heel and slammed the door of the study behind her. The noise made the bits of opaline on the floor tremble ever so slightly. Brigitte looked calmly at Paul.

"I've never seen my sister so nervous. What did you say that put her in such a state?"

"Nothing special, as far as I know. I think perhaps she mistook my deferential attitude for irony."

Brigitte remained unconvinced.

"What about the vase?" she suggested.

"Mrs. Proust was so insistent that I stop work immediately that I couldn't quite resist showing her one of the consequences."

"But why did she fire you?"

"She'll probably explain. Something to do with the laundry. But I think I should let her tell you."

"What a bother! It's so stupid. Everything was going so well. You can't leave, just like that. I'm sure there's some way to settle this."

Paul shook his head. "I doubt it."

"As soon as Simone calms down, I'll go and tell her—"

"The problem has nothing to do with Simone—I mean, Mrs. Proust."

"Then, who?"

"It's because of me. I'm so sorry to leave you high and dry like this. All modesty aside, I realize that you'll have difficulty replacing me. But circumstances force me to put an end to our association."

"What circumstances? If you need a few days off—"

"Thank you. I understand how you feel, but my mind is made up. Not to mention that your sister was the one who fired me and that under her roof—"

"She's always been like this! She never does

anything except take for granted that other people will run the house for her. Finally, when we find the perfect solution, she goes into a fit of temper and ruins everything."

"Oh, no. Not that I mean to excuse Mrs. Proust, since she's obviously hard to get along with, but I really must leave anyway. If you'll recall our first conversation, I told you I would be only a stopgap, and gave no promise as to how long I could stay."

"Fine. Then I'll go back home, and let Simone work things out on her own!"

"Oh, no. It would be a shame to ruin the children's holiday. Who knows? Maybe you'll find a maid."

Brigitte sighed and stared at Paul in puzzlement.

"You're certainly a strange one!"

Paul smiled at the remark.

"I simply try to put a little spice into life. And from time to time I take an interest in others."

"What do you mean?"

"You'll soon find out. But be sure not to let your imagination run away with you."

He consulted his watch.

"Excuse me. I'm expecting a telephone call at three o'clock. It's now two minutes to three, and since Mrs. Proust is in the study I think I should post myself next to the phone on the second floor."

He had scarcely finished climbing the stairs when the phone rang. Brigitte heard him say a few words in a low tone. A minute later he was back at her side.

"That's exactly what I was waiting for—confirmation that today would be my last. Please don't hold it against your sister. What happened just now had no effect on anything—except the vase, of course."

He bowed elegantly, causing Brigitte to wonder how, in the space of only a few minutes, he could use the same gesture to convey two feelings that were diametrically opposed.

"I'll be back to say goodbye to you and the children. In the meantime, I'll leave you the task of telling Diana that her mother is waiting for her."

Just as he was about to go out the door, he turned and added, "By the way, she'll probably need a couple of aspirins, too."

Chapter 14

By the time Diana reached the study, Simone had calmed down. Not wishing to compromise her chances of making her daughter listen to reason, she greeted Diana with a well-prepared smile.

"It's been a long time since we've had a chat, just the two of us."

Diana was already on the defensive since she was prepared for a heated struggle ending in a final break.

Brigitte had given her a few words of warning. "I don't know what's happening, but your mother's in a vile mood. She just fired Paul."

Diana hadn't shown one iota of surprise.

"That's not important. Anyway—"

"What?"

"Nothing. I'll explain later. You say she wants to talk to me? How convenient. I have a few things to say, myself. See you later."

And she strode off and almost marched down the stairs. But now that she was actually on the battlefield, she was embarrassed by the all-too-obvious trap that was her mother's smile.

She sat down rather stiffly, feeling as she had several years earlier when she'd been called before the headmistress of her boarding school.

"You never say anything. You're always so formal with me and—what's the word—distrustful. As if you were a child who expected to be punished."

Diana made a vague contradictory gesture and tried to look more relaxed. Simone went on.

"But I have no intention of criticizing you. In fact, it's just the opposite. Jack and I are delighted at the way you and Chamberland are getting along."

"Fine. But it doesn't mean much."

"What do you mean? You've been seeing each other every day for the past few weeks—"

"I'm doing as you asked, and nothing more."

"Well, if appearances are anything to go by, you aren't exactly bored by him."

"True. He's pleasant and intelligent, and more sensitive and cultured than I had expected."

"Good for you!"

"But it ends there."

"In other words?"

"In other words, in spite of all those fine qualities, I still don't feel anything for him."

Diana turned away, yet continued to speak, as if searching her soul aloud.

"I'm the first to be surprised. After all those hours spent with him, I still haven't felt even the slightest spark. Friendship, yes. I recognize all his good qualities and realize he's not bad looking, but . . . . I just don't know. . . . Something in him turns me to ice. He has no warmth, no depth of feeling. Even when he tries to kiss me, as he did last night, I can't help feeling that he's playing a part."

She looked up at her mother and added, "You'll never understand."

"That's exactly where you're wrong. I understand all too well, unfortunately." Simone observed her daughter carefully. "It's such a shame—" She sighed.

"Maybe, but there's nothing I can do about it."

"Expecially since the business is far from back on its feet."

"I'm sorry, but I've done everything I could. Remember what you asked me to do: to get to know him and give love a chance. And at the same time give you a reprieve—"

"It was an awfully short reprieve, don't you think?"

"I've discovered everything I need to know. Why prolong the experiment? Besides, Chamberland is getting more and more impatient. Last night he asked me to give him an answer. Up until now I've kept up the pretense and been able to help you out while at the same time being fairly true to myself. But I can't do that anymore, because I can't treat love as a game. It would be unfair to Chamberland, dangerous to me, and useless for you—"

"Useless! You have no idea how serious the situation is. How many times do I have to tell you: if he pulls out, we're ruined."

"And how many times do I have to tell you that I can't marry a man who means nothing to me? I'm sorry. I'd have been only too glad to fall in love with him, but as it turns out—"

"As it turns out, you prefer one of the servants!"

Her mother's unexpected words stung like the lash of a whip, but Diana recovered immediately. "Exactly, and I'm delighted you've finally discovered the truth."

"It was quite by accident, I assure you. I was going past the laundry room this morning and I happened to notice your little tête-à-tête."

"Fine. I was going to tell you about it, anyway."

"I'm not interested in your infatuations."

"It's not an infatuation. I'm in love with Paul."

"Really! And I suppose you intend to marry him?"

"Let's just say I'd like to."

Simone stood up quickly.

"There's no point in pursuing the matter. I think you must be completely out of your mind. He's not the one who'll get us out of this mess."

"But maybe he's the one who'll make me happy! I don't suppose that thought has ever occurred to you."

"How can he make you happy when he can't even give you the necessities of life?"

She walked around the desk to meet Diana, who had in turn risen to her feet.

"Listen to me, Diana. I just can't believe that a girl like you . . . . I'm the first to admit that he's good-looking and he has a certain charm. But, for heaven's sake, don't mistake this sort of attraction for the real thing!"

"You mean money? I'm sorry, mother, but we just don't see eye to eye on this. To me, money is useful but not essential."

"My God! I'd forgotten how stupid one can be at your age! We'll talk about this later, but in the meantime, I beg of you, wait just a little longer. What you feel for Paul is nothing more than a passing fancy. And by the way, to make things easier, I was obliged to fire him."

"I know. Brigitte told me. And it's a good thing, too. From now on you won't be able to reproach me for being in love with one of the servants."

The two women glared at each other and then Simone said coldly, "In a few months you'll be twenty-one and you'll be able to do all the asinine things you want. And if there's anything left of the business, you'll get the few crumbs you're entitled to. But I'd advise you to think things over and not pin your hopes on the first stranger you meet. Use the same approach with Paul as you did with Chamberland. And don't forget the world is full of parasites and fortune hunters with their eye on the main chance!"

Barely controlling her anger, Diana made no reply, but simply headed for the door. Just as she thought she had put an end to the conversation, her mother got in one last parting shot.

"Perhaps you should go over to the village."

"And why should I do that?"

"Just an idea. You know that little inn, on this side of the station . . . the one with the gardens?"

"Yes. What about it?"

"Well, I don't really know, but I have a feeling if you were there at about five o'clock, you might get a better idea of the sort of people this friend of yours keeps company with. . . ."

AN HOUR LATER Diana had borrowed Brigitte's car and was on her way to the village. Never had she felt so at odds with herself; she was disgusted with herself for taking her mother's suggestion, yet she couldn't resist the temptation.

She had tried in vain to come up with some excuse. After all, she couldn't deny that Paul's personality seemed to change like a chameleon and that his true nature was almost as much of a mystery now as it had been the first day. She had no idea who he really was or how he spent his time when he wasn't working as a servant.

What Diana wanted to know was what he became when he took off his gray shirt and blue apron and left the estate.

The conclusion she drew from this reasoning was that there was nothing wrong with observing him. Her interest was not only legitimate, but praiseworthy.

But all these fine reasons left her with an aftertaste of shameful regret. The word "observe" was nothing better than a euphemism. Diana might just as well have said "to spy on" Paul—which threw an entirely different light on what she was doing. In short, she was not at all proud of her decision.

Now she was asking herself how she could have neglected to ask her mother any questions. How could Simone know anything about Paul's private life when Diana herself had always been in the dark? And why was Simone interested in "the sort of people" he knew?

Diana had reached the outskirts of the village. She was tempted to turn around, for her feeling of regret was growing even stonger. It was wrong to be suspicious, especially when she had just admitted her love for him.

But curiosity got the better of her and she resolved to go through with her plan. She drove past the sign marking the beginning of the village proper and turned left onto the road leading to the station.

The inn her mother had mentioned had a charming name: The Lost Doe. It was a half-timbered building with cob walls and leaded-glass windows enhanced by boxes of geraniums in full bloom. It had a few rooms, usually rented to traveling salesmen, a small lounge, and a luxuriant garden.

The square was deserted since the evening train wasn't due until six o'clock. Diana parked her car and sat pensively at the wheel, trying to make up her mind. The Lost Doe looked exceedingly quiet. Through the open door she could just make out the cool shadowy interior. Through the gate on the right she could see white tables shaded by red umbrellas.

The station was just as calm. The rails gleamed brightly in the afternoon sun. The only sign of life was a chicken that had probably escaped from the stationmaster's poultry yard and was scratching about in the red gravel of the platform. An open pushcart rumbled across the square and out of sight.

Diana finally made up her mind. She got out of the car and began to stroll around. Then she told herself that an inn was a public place and that she had every right to go in for something to drink—especially when it was almost ninety degrees in the shade!

She went in, saw that the room was empty, and sat down at a table to wait. By now her throat was parched and she was dying for a cold drink, either because of the heat or because of her anxiety. But there was no one to be seen. Through the glassed door beyond the counter she glimpsed a white kitchen. Diana went over and saw that this room, too, was deserted, but that it led out to a large sunny courtyard.

This gave her the idea of going to the end of the room and taking a look out into the garden through a vine-covered window. But already her fears had been dispelled. She had arrived at five minutes to five; it was now a quarter past, and she hadn't seen anything out of the ordinary. Probably her mother had simply wanted to upset her with unfounded insinuations. She sighed with relief at the thought that she could put the ridiculous incident out of her mind.

But these comforting thoughts were abruptly banished. Diana stared at what she saw, her eyes wide with disbelief. Her heart stopped beating for a moment, only to start up again at a furious pace. Framed by one of the arbors in the garden was Paul. Paul in profile, leaning tenderly toward a face that at first was only a blur and then became that of a dark-haired young woman who was undeniably pretty.

Leaning toward each other, absorbed in conversation, they presented the perfect image of a young couple marveling at their newly found love.

She had learned all she wanted to know about Paul—

"Yes, miss?"

Diana jumped and wheeled around. A short, ruddy-cheeked waitress was looking at her in astonishment.

"Would you like something to drink?"

"No. I . . . . I just came in to see . . . to see if one of my friends was here. . . ."

Diana was angry at herself for sputtering out nonsense, and especially for blushing to the roots of her hair as if she were a naughty five-year-old. She added in a more assured tone of voice as she made for the door, "But she's not here and I don't have time to wait."

"Perhaps you're looking for the lady in the garden. She's with a gentleman. . . ."

Diana stopped. "Do you know her?"

"She's been here several times. Usually she takes one of the rooms. We give her the best one, next to the owners' room. But today she said she's taking the six o'clock train back to Paris."

"And the gentleman? Has he been here before, too?" Diana's voice was choked.

"Every time!"

The waitress's tone of voice spoke volumes, for it undoubtedly categorized Paul and the beautiful stranger as an official couple. Diana felt as if her heart had been locked in a painful vise.

"She's not the woman I'm looking for. But thank you anyway," she muttered as she stumbled out the door.

"No trouble at all," the waitress called after her.

As she walked back to the car, Diana could feel unshed tears threatening to overcome her. *I won't cry*, she vowed. *I won't cry*. She hastily started the car and shot away. Behind her The Lost Doe disappeared in a cloud of dust, while ahead of her the road became almost indiscernible through the rain of tears she could no longer hold back.

Chapter 15

Diana dreamed that she was riding toward Templars'
Crossing. The forest was as it once had been. The
beeches had mysteriously reappeared with their
smooth trunks and canopy of colored leaves. It was
autumn and a profusion of copper and gold tones
sang their song to the sky.

Prince had been by her side only a moment ago, but
had disappeared. Diana was not upset, however. She
lay down among the ferns at the foot of a tree. She was
tired and sad, yet she didn't know why since she had
rediscovered the forest of her childhood.

And then, way up in the tree, a green woodpecker
began tapping so insistently and with such strength
that Diana had to leave the tree because each tap resounded painfully in her mind. . . .

At that moment she had the feeling she was not
alone. A silhouette appeared in the dim light of the
undergrowth. She suddenly sat up . . . and found
herself in her bedroom, stretched out on a chaise

longue. She saw her grandmother standing before her with a smile on her face.

"You were really fast asleep! I knocked for a good minute, but couldn't get any answer. I was beginning to get worried."

"I took a pill so that I could get to sleep. With this heat it's the best way to kill time."

"I think I've found another. Caroline got it into her head that she wants to go to the seashore. And you know how it is once she has her heart set on something. . . ."

"But the beaches are probably jammed with people."

"We're going to try to find a quiet spot. Besides, don't you think it's a good idea to mingle with a crowd once in a while, if only to come back more appreciative of the peace and quiet here?"

"Personally, I appreciate it enough as it is."

"I know, and that's what worries me. It isn't right to spend so much time alone at your age. Why, you haven't come out of your room for the past three days."

"I'm tired. And it's too hot to run around in the woods."

"I agree. But wouldn't you like a nice swim?"

"Sorry, gran. I'd rather stay here."

"Brigitte will be disappointed. She feels as if you've abandoned her."

"But Brigitte has the children. She doesn't need me to keep her company."

Mrs. Faber observed her granddaughter with tender concern. Diana had turned away. She was sitting in the shadow of the window blind, but it was still easy to see that there were circles under her eyes and that she was very pale.

"Are you sure you don't want to come with us?"

Diana forced a tired smile.

"No, gran. I'm sorry, but I really do feel like having a nap."

"All right. I won't insist. Have a good rest, but don't forget that you still need to get out once in a while."

When she was halfway to the door, she turned and said, "Oh, I'd forgotten. I have a favor to ask of you. I've an errand to run tonight. Would you mind driving me?"

"Of course not, gran, but—"

"Because we're going out this afternoon, Brigitte will have to do the ironing after dinner. Now that we have no one . . . ."

And then she added in a low tone of voice, "One more thing. I know it sounds strange, but please don't say anything about tonight in front of your mother. I don't want her to ask any questions. I'll explain later."

Diana listened as her grandmother's footsteps died away. Shortly afterward she heard her little cousins shouting gleefully under her window and the car starting up. Then silence closed in around her. She sighed, leaned back, and shut her eyes.

Now she would be able to remain alone, undisturbed until dinner. As she had done yesterday and the day before, she would spend the long empty hours lying motionless, her body languid and her mind emptied of all thoughts, almost as if she had released her grip on life. It was the best way to avoid suffering, for though she knew she had been hurt, she still had not let herself think about just how much.

Perhaps one day this interval would no longer count. At some point Diana would rediscover her love of life and desire for activity. But until then she wished to do only one thing: to be alone with the drapes closed, to rest in the shadows, neither speaking nor listening to anyone.

At least she was fortunate in one respect; her mother and stepfather almost never spoke to her. And Chamberland had not shown his face at the estate since the night of the infamous party. As for Paul, he had most likely taken the train along with his beautiful friend, since no one had seen him since the day he left them.

Oh, why had she let herself be taken in by him?

Her mother's warning rang in her ears: "Don't forget the world is full of parasites and fortune hunters with their eye on the main chance."

Although Diana had originally bridled at this comment, she was now forced to admit to herself that it probably did correspond to reality after all. How painful it was merely to think of his name. How she wished she could wipe the image of his smile from her memory and forget his voice. And then there were the burning kisses that she could still feel on her lips. The mere thought of them was enough to start her trembling.

Diana closed her eyes once more as tears welled up in them. She must not cry, she told herself, because Paul was not worth it. And after all, time would attenuate her pain, just as it heals all wounds—even those inflicted by first love. In a few weeks or months she would be the first to smile at her infatuation.

But in the meantime, there were pills that brought sleep and drapes that offered protection from the cruel summer sun. In that way she did her best to push away all thoughts and to slip into a world where nothing remained of life except the low hum of a million insects dancing in the heat.

"WHERE ARE WE GOING?"

"First to the village. From there I'll direct you."

The car rolled smoothly through the main gates of the estate. Diana asked no further questions. In spite of the fact that her grandmother was obviously up to something mysterious, she was not the least bit interested, let alone intrigued. All her pain and suffering had dissolved into a state of benumbed serenity that actually masked profound despair.

If this state of body and mind were to continue, perhaps it would not be so hard to go on living at all. For she felt that her heart was dead, and that if she was incapable of experiencing any joy, she was also immune to suffering. It would be almost akin to living under permanent anesthesia.

But at any moment was she not likely to wake up screaming with the pain? She shook away the thoughts.

"I'm glad we have the chance to talk to each other alone, gran. For the past two months, we've been almost strangers to each other."

"That's true. Sometimes we're a bit like two people staying in a hotel who see each other only at mealtime. But it's normal, because you're young and you have your own life to lead and your own preoccupations."

"And you're always afraid of imposing on me, aren't you?"

"That's what you accused me of doing one day. Do you remember?"

"That was the night Celine quit. We talked about mother and the business . . . and Chamberland. Since then things have changed, but not for the better, unfortunately!"

Mrs. Faber stared straight ahead at the road without offering any comment. In the beams of light cast by the headlights of the car, they could see hundreds of tiny toads.

"The same night mother told me about her worries, she strongly recommended that I fall in love with Chamberland if I wanted to put an end to our problems. . . ."

"I know. Brigitte told me about it."

Diana sensed that her words contained a reproach. She said, "I didn't want to get you mixed up in it and have you at odds with mother. And I thought it over and decided that since there was nothing you could do, anyway. . . ."

"As far as Simone and Jack were concerned I couldn't. . . . But go on with what you were saying."

"Dutiful daughter that I am, I agreed to go out with Chamberland and get to know him better in the hope that I might fall in love with him. Of course, nothing of the kind happened. But now I've resigned myself to marrying him, anyway. And that's that. This time, you're the first one to hear the news."

Diana glanced expectantly at her passenger, but no reaction was forthcoming. Instead, Mrs. Faber simply said, "I had a feeling you'd finally arrive at that decision."

This time it was Diana's turn to be surprised. It was unthinkable that her grandmother had so little to say, that she hadn't even uttered a word of protest against such a sacrifice. There had not even been a trace of sympathy in her voice.

Diana went on doggedly, "And I plan to marry him as soon as possible. It's high time we were solvent again. I visited Emilie this afternoon and she told me that mother's planning to sell Hazel Farms. I suppose it was that news that swept away any hesitations I had. Because of my selfishness, soon even Emilie would be out of a home."

As Mrs. Faber remained silent, Diana began to regret having confided in her. She smiled bitterly at the thought that no one seemed to care a scrap about her happiness.

The car rolled on, rounding one bend after another. The roadway was still strewn with toads, tiny dancing spots on the pavement, fascinating to the eye.

When they reached the village, Diana asked, "Should I drop you off somewhere?"

"No. Turn right at the church and take the road to Williamsburg."

Diana's heart began to beat faster. It was on this road, only a few days earlier that Paul had stopped the car and under a starry sky . . . . Diana quickly decided she must say something, anything, to banish this memory from her thoughts.

"Williamsburg?" she asked in surprise. "Andrew lives over in this direction."

"I know. I hadn't found the right moment to tell you, but that's where we're going."

"To Andrew's? Now? Whatever for?"

Diana shifted gears without thinking, and the car gathered speed as it left the sleepy village. Mrs. Faber replied, "Well, let's just say I'd like to get to know him better. It's the least I can do, don't you think? Since you intend to marry the man . . . ."

"WHAT'S THE POINT of this?" asked Andrew Chamberland.

Proust shrugged. "I was just about to ask you the same thing."

There was a trace of amusement in his voice, probably because his partner was reacting with such nervousness.

"My mother-in-law didn't say a word to me, except to be at your place at nine o'clock. I thought you knew why she arranged this . . . meeting."

"She just telephoned this morning to say that she was coming over . . . without any explanation, as if she were a teacher announcing something to a student. You can imagine how I felt about that."

Chamberland's office opened directly onto the garden. It was furnished with leather-upholstered armchairs and bound volumes, as well as an antique Norman sideboard housing a beautiful collection of Jersey pottery.

On a small marble and wrought-iron table were bottles of cognac and calvados. Chamberland had already emptied his glass twice and begun chain smoking. Proust, on the other hand, was much more calm.

"You actually looked worried," he commented ironically, "even though 'formidable' is a word I'd never use to describe Mrs. Faber. Look at me! I'm her son-in-law and I'm not trembling in my boots.'

Chamberland looked at him darkly.

"I'm furious, if you want to know the truth. She doesn't even have the decency to arrive on time. I find her whole attitude extremely offhand."

Ignoring Chamberland's outburst, Proust remarked, "Personally, one thing does puzzle me—the way she left Simone out of this completely. I really don't see what kind of conversation my wife shouldn't hear."

"I don't, either, but we'll soon find out. I hear a car."

"I wonder who could have brought her here. She doesn't know how to drive."

Proust's question was answered almost immediately. When he saw Diana at the wheel, Chamberland's face relaxed and his worries seemed to vanish. Yet he was still on the defensive when he showed the two visitors in without a word, and sat down at his desk expectantly.

Mrs. Faber refused the armchair offered her.

"I won't stay long," she announced. "I'm sure that a man such as you, Mr. Chamberland, will understand what brings me here, without my having to draw pictures."

"It depends on the subject."

"Obviously. Accordingly, I'll come straight to the point."

"Perhaps you'll also tell me why you asked your son-in-law to come, too, without mentioning it to me."

"I thought it was the best way to arrange things. He's your friend, isn't he? What I have to say concerns him as much as it does you. In a minute or two you'll understand better."

Mrs. Faber spoke in a gentle, almost apologetic voice, that was completely at variance with her character. Diana and Proust, who had sat down outside the circle of light cast by the lamp on the desk, felt uneasy at her tone and wondered what the meaning of her visit could be. Chamberland also felt a strange unease touch him and his nervousness returned once more. He began to twist an elastic band around in his hand.

"The purpose of my visit is to give you some good news," continued Mrs. Faber. "All things taken into account—" she broke off and gave a short laugh before continuing "—the expression really is very apt—Diana has decided to marry you."

Chamberland remained impassive, but Proust started slightly and Diana felt a sinking feeling in the pit of her stomach. Her decision, said out loud, seemed irrevocable somehow.

"But it's true, my dear Jack. Your stepdaughter is much more realistic than you think. Your arguments finally convinced her. Isn't that right, Diana?"

Not waiting for a reply, she turned back to Chamberland.

"Personally, I have nothing against the marriage. But I want her to enter into it with both eyes wide open, and for that reason I'd like to help the two of you to get better acquainted with each other. It's the least a grandmother can do, don't you think?"

"Just what are you getting at?" Chamberland barked.

"Well . . . what I just told you. Why are you looking at me like that? You look—how should I put it—as if you don't trust me."

"I see no reason for that."

"Neither do I. In any case, it's inevitable that Diana would discover the truth sooner or later—"

"The truth about what?"

"About your agreement—if you can call it that—with my son-in-law. In other words, the real part you play in the bankruptcy of Cavalier Textiles."

"I don't think I quite understand—"

"How strange! Perhaps I'm mistaken. But judging by the expression on your friend Jack's face, I think he gets the point."

Proust was ashen. From where he sat stiffly in his corner of the room, he stared at his mother-in-law. She gestured reassuringly at him.

"Now, now. Let's not be overly dramatic. Business is business. I know you'd prefer to have Simone here, but I thought it would be better to discuss these things without her. What's the point in telling her, if we can spare her the pain?"

"Tell her what?" asked Chamberland, leaning forward.

Now that the first shock had worn off, he was ready to make a stand. His eyes gleamed knowingly. If Mrs. Faber noticed, she didn't let on, but instead continued to speak in her slightly hesitant voice, as if she didn't want to offend anyone.

"I'm sorry." She sighed, shaking her head. "I was counting on you to make things easier. How mistaken one can be! It was so naive of me to think we would simply lay our cards on the table. It would have saved me from a most embarrassing explanation."

"Explanation of what?" Chamberland snapped.

Mrs. Faber eyed him coldly. Her hesitant manner dropped from her like a tiresome cloak. "Very well, have it your way."

She sank into the armchair that she had refused on arrival.

"In the beginning, I believed, like Simone and Diana, that you and Jack were really business associates, both doing your best to make the company a success. After all, that was the official version. The only problem was that the business began to fail. When my first son-in-law was alive, it was a healthy, expanding company. All of a sudden it's very existence was in jeopardy. The explanations you furnished—fierce competition and over investment—were ingenious, but not terribly convincing. I think I know enough to be able to judge a man, and I have far too much respect for you—on the professional level, of course—not to be surprised at the pitiful results. Jack is a hard worker, and you, Mr. Chamberland, are a fine accountant and ₑ remarkable businessman. But in spite of that, the Cavalier business has been going downhill for the last ten years and now it's on the verge of bankruptcy. How do you explain that?"

Chamberland was still twisting the elastic around his hand. Yet he seemed to have regained complete control of himself. He stared icily at the tiny woman in black seated before him.

"The laws of the economy often work in mysterious ways," he declared, apparently in complete seriousness.

Mrs. Faber began to laugh.

"The economy has nothing to do with it! It's much simpler than that. The Cavalier business would have flourished, Mr. Chamberland, had not all its profits found their way into your pockets!"

"Because of Jack's generosity, no doubt?"

"Because you were blackmailing him." Mrs. Faber's eyes were flaming, and her face mirrored her contempt.

"I think you owe me an explanation!" Chamberland's face was flushed.

"I owe you nothing except a one-way ticket to jail. And if my daughter refuses to take action—"

Chamberland leaned forward in his chair. "This is absurd," he declared angrily. "You aren't making any sense at all. Why don't you admit it: you don't want me to marry Diana, so you've invented this cock-and-bull story!"

"You're wrong. I haven't invented a thing! It's all there: Jack's tampering with the accounts, your covering it up. . . . You were talking about it not too long ago in the study at the estate. Don't you remember? It was just after you got back from your business trip."

Chamberland, frowning like a man who smells a rat, turned his gaze on Proust, who was staring at his mother-in-law, dumbfounded. Mrs. Faber smiled ironically.

"Look no farther," she said in answer to their silent questions. "It's understandable that you may have forgotten the details, so I've arranged to refresh your memory. . . ."

As she spoke, something extraordinary happened. She was interrupted by the voice of Chamberland himself, but it came through an open door connecting the study to the next room. "Look at this sunlit park and all your fine horses. Without me, Proust, you'd be looking at something entirely different; you'd be rotting away, forgotten, in some prison."

Then Proust spoke in his weak, toneless voice.

"Don't be ridiculous. It wouldn't have gone that far."

The two men jumped to their feet. Diana stiffled the cry of surprise that almost escaped her lips.

The voices continued. "Do you want me to look it up in the criminal code for you?" retorted Chamberland. "Breach of trust, forgery, embezzlement. . . . You'd have been lucky to get off with ten years!"

Mrs. Faber was wreathed in smiles.

"There you are," she declared. "What you forgot to mention that day—"

But Chamberland wasn't listening to her. He rushed over to the communicating door, but stopped dead as a tall silhouette appeared to block his path. It was Paul on his way into the study, with a tape recorder in his hand.

"Going somewhere, Mr. Chamberland?"

Then he casually went over and deposited the tape recorder on the desk. He switched the machine on and Chamberland's voice resounded throughout the room.

"Thanks to my skill as an accountant, I not only corrected the situation, but turned it around in your favor, attributing all the losses to Cavalier's so-called mismanagement—"

Paul shook his head disapprovingly as he switched off the tape.

"Tsk, tsk! Now that's not nice at all! I wonder what the police would think about the way you put your accounting skills to use?"

Chamberland no longer looked like a suave and controlled businessman. He was white with rage. His lips trembled and the convulsive movements of his fingers betrayed his futile attempts to keep himself in check.

"Wha-what are *you* doing here?" Chamberland demanded.

Paul looked at him mildly. "Don't worry. Lucky for you your friend Reynolds didn't send me. Come to think of it, I don't even know the man."

Chamberland seemed about to choke. "But—but you said—"

Paul interrupted. "Yes, well, I lied. You see, I once overheard a very interesting conversation at a village inn. It made me curious about the speakers, and I became even more curious when I recognized one of the speakers driving off with a lovely young girl. I could have ignored the warning signals in my head, or I could have become involved. I decided on the latter course."

Proust spoke up, "What the devil is he talking about, Chamberland?"

Chamberland shrugged in reply.

Paul continued, "I began working at the estate as a servant, and it didn't take me long to discover that the Proust-Chamberland friendship was nothing but a facade. Only a servant—that is, someone insignificant, in whose presence you don't always remember to play your role—is able to see certain telltale expressions and glances. One day I got the idea to put this little tape recorder in the study and connect it to a switch I had installed on the other side of the wall in place of a buzzer that no longer worked. . . ."

He smiled and bowed slightly to Mrs. Faber.

"You arrived just as I finished. Admit that I had you worried that day!"

"Well, curious would be a better word. But I could tell you were on my side."

She pointed out the recorder. "And then you proved it a few days later when you brought me this tape."

Chamberland said, "All this is extremely interesting, but I don't quite see what you're getting at. I suppose you had something in mind when you arranged this little scene?"

"You're right, Mr. Chamberland," replied Mrs. Faber. "I came with specific objectives in mind. First, I want Diana to be able to see you as you really are. This, I think, has been accomplished. Second, I want to know how you plan to give back what you've 'deducted' from the business."

Chamberland laughed. "You're incredibly naive! What should I give back, and why?"

"Because if you don't, you'll have a great deal of trouble on your hands!" Paul replied.

"Would you care to elaborate?"

"All right. First, we reveal your little plan to Mrs. Proust—"

"That won't exactly help her marriage, will it?"

"Perhaps not, but knowing her as I do, I predict she won't have a moment's hesitation about pressing charges for embezzlement, forgery, and all the rest. Then, an inquiry will be opened, and when all the records dating from Alan Cavalier's death to the present are examined, it will come out into the open that the eminent Andrew Chamberland, gentleman farmer, chartered accountant and financial advisor, is in reality nothing more than a master blackmailer and crook!"

"Do you really think so? One of my best friends is a lawyer who'll have no trouble drawing just the opposite conclusion! You're the babe in the woods when it comes to the business world. It all depends on how you present your facts. Besides, all my transcations with Proust were carried out with due respect to the law."

"Really? Even when you juggled the books to get him out of that mess?"

"You can't prove anything!"

"I can." Mrs. Faber spoke up. "I spent several nights cross-checking the books with the accountant at the plant. We came across several documents of particular interest."

Certain telltale signs betrayed Chamberland's tenseness—the rapid blinking of his eyes, the fidgeting movement of his hands, and the combative note in his voice.

"It's absurd. If things went that far, your son-in-law would be finished. Simone wouldn't do that to her own husband. It would create a scandal from here to Paris."

"Faced with the choice between poverty and a scandal, she wouldn't hesitate a minute," Paul remarked.

"You've forgotten one thing, Mr. Chamberland," put in Mrs. Faber. "My granddaughter will be twenty-one in a few months and she'll demand a complete account of the matter."

"Oh, I think our friend is well aware of Diana's age," observed Paul. "That's one of the main reasons he wanted to marry her. Once he was married, he'd have nothing left to fear. But that was only one of the reasons. The desire to worm his way once and for all into a respectable upper-class family was another."

He went over to Chamberland and looked him in the eye.

"It would have been useful, wouldn't it? First you feather your nest, then you do everything you can to cover up your not-so-honorable past. Do you want me to go into details?"

The two men glared at each other and then Chamberland turned to Mrs. Faber and asked, "What do you want from me?"

"I've already told you: all the property you've acquired over the last ten years. That's all."

"Really? I doubt we'll be able to come to an agreement," Chamberland said through clenched teeth. "I have no intention of giving up what is legally mine."

"We don't care what you intend," put in Paul.

"No court of law will take it away from me! All the contracts and deeds of transfer are in perfect order."

Mrs. Faber gestured wearily. "That may well be, but you still have to account to us."

"And in your position, it could be very sticky. Imagine what your friends will think when they see your real name in the newspapers," Paul murmured.

"What do you mean?" Chamberland's face went suddenly pale.

"When they ask you whether you're really Lindemann, alias Chamberland. When they find out that when you were in your twenties you served several years for smuggling drugs."

"That's not true!"

"You gave yourself away the night I came to get Diana and said your name and told you I was a friend of Reynolds's! And you're giving yourself away at this very moment. If you could only see yourself!"

Chamberland had turned chalky white. He was staring at Paul with a mixture of fear and hatred.

"That night I didn't have all the details, but your reaction confirmed my suspicions. And the next day Cecile Chamberland gave me the proof that I needed. Does that name mean anything to you?"

Diana stifled a gasp. Was that the name of the woman Paul had met?

While he paced back and forth, he explained to Diana and Proust, "Cecile Chamberland is no relation to our friend here. She's a charming young woman who recently married, and her name is now Cecile Gall. In any case, her father, Roy Chamberland, was an accountant and real-estate broker with offices in Paris. When he died about ten years ago, Lindemann bought his business from behind the scenes, and retained the name, but wisely stepped to one side. That is, until the day he decided it would be safe to show himself once more using the name Chamberland, the one his clients were accustomed to calling him by. Here I should add that our friend, as was to be expected, managed to wiggle out of his promises to the Chamberland family—legally, of course—thereby saving himself huge sums of money. With the result that Cecile was delighted to join forces with us, give us access to her family's files, and do everything that had to be done in Paris. In return, we agreed to help her recover every penny owed to her."

"How did you find out all that?" Chamberland asked after several moments' silence.

This time Mrs. Faber answered.

"What does any woman do when she has to get information about someone? First, she consults a lawyer, who advises her that without proof there's no way she can press charges—especially when her opponent is someone like you! So the only solution is to hire a private detective. I was surprised at the amount of information he gathered, but without Paul's help I wouldn't have been able to do much with it. Your past didn't really concern me. And I couldn't press charges against you using your police record as the reason. You had money and connections in high places. . . . In short, your past was dead and your new social status hard to strip away."

Again she pointed to the tape recorder.

"I needed this tape to be able to prove that you were blackmailing my son-in-law and embezzling money from the company. It enables me to meet you on your terms and blackmail you in my own way."

Chamberland's eyes blazed. He glanced at the tape recorder still sitting on the desk. In one swift movement, he lunged forward.

Misinterpreting Chamberland's intent, Paul reached across and swept the tape recorder off the desk. But Chamberland's movement had carried him to the top drawer in his desk. A gun was in his hand when he whirled to face the others.

"My God, Andrew—" Jack Proust exclaimed.

"Shut up, you imbecile!" Chamberland's voice was gritty. Now he leveled the gun at Paul. "I don't know who the hell you really are, but you've been a thorn in my side for long enough. Get against the wall."

Paul stood his ground. "Don't be a fool, Chamberland. What are you going to do? Shoot all of us?"

Chamberland's smile was a cold grimace. "You're the one who is the fool. A meddlesome fool. Look around you. You see the results of generations of French aristocracy; these people are family. They'll stick together through thick and thin. They won't turn me in and wash their dirty linen in public—"

"Andrew! What are—" Diana exclaimed.

"Shut up!" Chamberland rapped. "Now where was

I? Oh, yes. Our meddlesome servant. You see, my friend," Chamberland addressed Paul, "you're an outsider. You might get ideas about going to the police—or lining your own pockets like Reynolds did. Once I'm rid of you, I have nothing to fear. Nothing at all."

Slowly, deliberately, Chamberland raised the gun.

"No!" Diana screamed, and lunged across the room.

For a split second Chamberland was distracted and in that instant, Paul sprang at him.

A shot rang out, and the acrid smell filled the air.

Diana watched, horrified, as Paul grappled with Chamberland, twisting the gun out of his hand. It fell beyond the reach of the two men. Had Paul been hit? Suddenly Chamberland seemd to gain the upper hand. He rolled on top of Paul and landed a blow to the younger man's jaw.

Stunned, Paul lashed out at Chamberland's face, grazing him.

Unable to stand by and do nothing, Diana flung herself on Chamberland's back, pushing the man off balance.

"Diana!" screamed Mrs. Faber, hurrying forward.

But Paul had recovered. He reached out and jerked on Chamberland's collar. Then with grim determination, he landed a blow that left his opponent senseless.

Struggling to his feet, Paul pulled Diana to hers and held her in his arms.

"Oh, Paul, you're all right," she murmured, then fainted.

Chapter 16

"Do you really think, Dr. Bergart, that these three pills—was it two or three? It's already slipped my mind."

"Three, every day. It's written on your prescription."

"Do you think they'll do any good?"

"Of course, ma'am. That's why I prescribed them. But for them to be effective, you must watch your diet carefully."

"All right. So I'm to come back and see you again in three weeks—was it two weeks or three?"

"A month. Give the medicine time to take effect. . . ."

The door finally closed behind her. Paul Bergart leaned back and lighted a cigarette with a sigh. His last patient of the day had certainly got her money's worth out of him.

Then it occurred to him that she might not actually be the last. It would be best to make a last check. His office hours had long since ended, but in the countryside it was impossible to make hard and fast rules. The young man peeked into the waiting room and did his best not to grimace at the sight of a woman dressed in black seated with her back to the window.

"Madam . . . ."

Because she was in the shadows, he didn't recognize her at first. As he stepped aside to let her pass, she said, "I'm sorry to be so late, but I've come a long way just to consult you."

"Mrs. Faber!"

Paul suddenly grew pale and stopped, his hand on the doorknob.

"You don't look very pleased to see me!"

"I'm . . . surprised. I really wasn't expecting . . . . But how did you find me?"

"I'm used to making inquiries, or had you forgotten? But this time, I didn't need to hire a detective. All I had to do was go to the little inn in the village where you stayed. Shall we go into your office? I really do wish to consult you."

With its freshly waxed red tile floor and beamed ceiling, the room still retained its rustic charm in spite of its being a doctor's office. Next to Paul, Mrs. Faber looked very tiny. She took his arm and scrutinized his face.

"You look tired. And you've lost weight."

"I've been working hard. Usually my father and I divide up the patients, but he took his vacation, so for several weeks I had to see them all."

Mrs. Faber shook her head with a smile.

"You never cease to amaze me! It had occurred to me that you might be a salesman, a journalist or a lawyer, or that perhaps you did nothing at all. But to find you working as a doctor in a small village—especially after hiring you as a servant."

"I can explain—"

"There's no need. Not now, anyway. We have all the time in the world to get acquainted. But I would like to know why you vanished into thin air a month ago."

The young man gestured evasively. For the first time he seemed ill at ease, if not intimidated. He was like a schoolboy called before the principal to explain an absence.

"My vacation was over, and since you didn't need me anymore—"

"But just the same, Paul . . . after everything you did for us!"

"Let's not exaggerate. Anyway, I don't see how you could have explained my presence to Mrs. Proust. I'm sure she'll never be able to think of me as anything but a servant whom she fired."

"But what it boils down to is that you left because of my granddaughter."

"In a sense . . . ."

"You were wrong to go. We could have found something to tell Simone. She's so superficial that she believes almost anything that you tell her. She's proved it time and again since that memorable evening at Chamberland's house!"

"Yes, I know."

"But how?"

."Well, I wanted to know whether Chamberland had come through."

"So?"

"So, last week, I dropped in to see Fernand."

"What?"

"He had invited me and I didn't want to hurt his feelings. He told me that he couldn't make head nor tail of it, and that everything had fallen into place as if by magic. He said not only was there no longer any talk of selling, but everything had been brought back in one fell swoop and that Simone thought it was some sort of a miracle."

"It's true. Chamberland wasted no time. The very next day after you disappeared he went to see Jack at the factory. All the transactions seem to be going smoothly. Believe it or not, he's even selling his home in Williamsburg."

"The place must bring back a lot of unhappy memories. But why don't we sit down? I'll tell mother—"

Mrs. Faber shook her head.

"Not right now. I'd love to meet your mother, but first tell me—if you saw Fernand, he must have told you how the family was—Brigitte, Simone, Jack . . . ?"

"Yes, of course. He told me everyone was well."

"Really. Even Diana?"

"Well . . . ."

"Perhaps her name didn't come up?"

"Listen—"

"Well, I've come to tell you exactly how she is. The consultation that I've come for is for her, not me."

"But—"

"Diana is not well at all. She's lost almost as much weight as you. Except that since she only weighed about two-thirds of your weight to begin with, it's even more noticeable. We simply must do something."

Paul gave no reply. He merely stared at Mrs. Faber with a strange, almost frightened look on his face.

"Can't you see? What's the point of giving her back her forest and her fortune if she's only going to pine away? Admit that your behavior has been anything but logical! Just because of her, you give up your vacation; instead of relaxing on a beach as you had planned, you get a job as a servant. You spend weeks mopping and dusting to save her from complete ruin and a forced marriage. And the very night you accomplish all this before we even have the chance to thank you, you rush off without leaving any address."

Paul had bowed his head under this torrent of words. More than ever he looked like a guilty child. Mrs. Faber went on, this time more casually. "Bear in mind that Diana can only conclude that you have your reasons for behaving like this."

"What reasons?"

"Well, you could be engaged or even married."

"Me? Never! Where did she get that idea?"

"You know how romantic young women let their imaginations run away with them. That day you met Cecile Gall, Diana saw the two of you and immediately jumped to the conclusion . . . ."

Paul's eyes grew wide with surprise.

"She saw us? Impossible! Who could have told her?"

"Probably her mother."

"But how did she know?"

"Brigitte and I asked ourselves that very question.

We came to the conclusion that Cecile must have telephoned you and arranged some kind of meeting."

"She did. I went up to the second floor to answer the phone."

"And Simone picked up the receiver and eaves-dropped on your conversation."

Paul stared at the toes of his shoes. All his assurance had vanished. He was a changed man!

"So Diana thought . . ." he muttered.

Mrs. Faber nodded gravely.

"And since you left for Paris right away to put things in order . . . ."

"Was she upset?"

"She didn't come out of her room for three days. Finally she decided to marry Chamberland as a sort of long-term suicide pact with herself."

"And now?"

"She spends every day in the forest. She comes home exhausted and goes straight to her room after dinner."

"Perhaps it's the shock of learning that Chamberland wasn't the man she thought he was."

"Pardon me?"

"I said, perhaps she's upset and disappointed about Chamberland?"

Mrs. Faber looked amazed. She stared at Paul to be sure he was serious.

"That never would have crossed my mind," she murmured. "Being in love must damage one's power of reasoning!"

Then she changed her tone of voice.

"So, have you finished playing hide and seek with yourself? What's the point of this little game? Diana's miserable and so are you! Is it because of your pride or because you're afraid of marriage? Your mother told me—"

"My mother?"

"Yes, your mother. You don't think I'd come without taking the necessary precautions. I wrote to her and received a long reply, all about how worried she was, how you had no appetite, how you used to be happy, but now always go around with a long face. Perhaps it's because of Cecile? I might as well tell you, she's very much in love with her husband."

For the first time since the conversaion had begun, Paul's face relaxed into a smile. It was the smile of a young boy who is both grateful and relieved that the principal has excused him.

"You're in love with Diana, aren't you?"

He nodded as if to indicate that it went without saying.

"But not enough to marry her?"

"That's not it at all! It's just the opposite!"

"Then what's stopping you?"

"I'm not rich."

"Listen, Paul, please don't make me waste my time proving your stupidity. If it weren't for you, Diana wouldn't have a cent to her name."

"It would still be more than what I could give her."

"But surely you're not serious? A doctor like you with a large practice—"

"We're the exception that proves the rule. About half of our patients never pay at all; it's a bad habit my father taught them."

"But you don't have to be like him."

"I don't think you understand. If I made them pay,

they'd be hard pressed to find the money. Some of them wouldn't even come back."

It took several seconds for his words to sink in. Finally she murmured, "That would be a shame. But that's beside the point. Diana doesn't care about how much money you make or how many patients you have—"

She broke off and cocked an ear.

"I can hear someone in your waiting room. You must still have patients to see. I don't want to hold you up."

"At this hour? I hardly think so."

"Don't you think you should at least check?"

As she pushed him toward the door, she added, "Just think, it might be someone who'll actually pay you."

From her smile and the way she looked at him, Paul understood what was really happening. He hesitated, as if searching for something to say, then turned on his heel, and rushed into the hallway.

Mrs. Faber closed the door and sat down in an armchair.

Diana was sitting by the window where her grandmother had been only a few minutes earlier. When she saw Paul in the doorway, she got to her feet and stood motionless, almost as if at attention. Under any other circumstances he would have quipped, "At ease!" but this time he walked over to her in silence and stopped with a small expectant smile.

It seemed that they stood looking at each other for an eternity, although in reality only a few seconds elapsed. They gazed questioningly into each other's eyes as a mysterious sense of calm took hold of them.

"You're thinner," murmured Paul, and then he added softly, "I'm sorry."

Diana shrugged a little to show that it didn't matter. She smiled in turn. Only a few words had succeeded in breaking down the barrier separating the two of them. They both relaxed and breathed more easily. Paul's assurance came back to him, although his voice still held a note of timidity.

"Your grandmother thinks I can put roses in your cheeks and give you back your appetite. I'm not sure I can, but I must try."

"Paul . . . ."

She sensed that he was about to take her in his arms and had already abandoned herself to her feelings. But instead, he declared in a professional tone of voice, "Morning and night, before meals, vitamin B12 and tonic for—"

"Paul!"

"And if that isn't enough, we'll have to try a long-term cure, one that's much more demanding and painful."

"What's that?"

"Marriage. Do you have any idea what that means? It's a very old remedy used to combat serious illnesses such as falling in love—"

"That's exactly—"

"I know what you're going to say. Since we have the same disease there's no danger of contaminating each other, so we might as well share our suffering."

"And our joys, too. I'm not really the courageous type, so I'd prefer to be happy, if it's all right with you."

"Then you'd best go see another doctor."

"I don't want another. I have confidence in you."

The shadows in the garden were tinged with copper, and the lawn strewn with dry leaves. Diana took Paul's hand and led him over to the window.

"I had to find you again before autumn came. I've never been so sad and lonely!"

At that moment a feeling of guilt swept over Paul. He took Diana in his arms and she leaned her face against his chest.

"If it hadn't been for grandmother, I never would have dared to come, and we would have spent the rest of our lives apart."

"No. We would have found each other again."

"Even though we live two hundred miles from each other?"

"I was on your estate last week."

"You came back?"

"To visit Fernand. I couldn't bear not knowing how you were. I left in the morning and came back that evening. I spent several hours by the pond, hoping to discover what I found the very first day—my little princess on the white horse. But it was raining, and all I came back with was my sadness, a dozen mushrooms, and a cold."

"That must be the only day I haven't gone to the pond since you left. But that doesn't matter, because I'm glad that I've taken the first step. I'm glad I came to get you at your house—"

"To get me?"

Paul had suddenly grown uneasy. "I can't quite picture myself living with Proust and your mother."

"They're going to move to Rouen. Mother is fed up with the country. But in any case, I don't plan to stay there—at least not right now."

"How can you give up Prince, and your little house, and your forest?"

"They'll mean all the more when we feel like riding . . . or swimming in the pond."

"Does that mean you'll live here?"

"Yes. Because I want to live with you, in your house, among the things that you love . . . ."

They fell silent. Diana sensed that Paul was about to object. She waited for his reasons so that she could burst them like soap bubbles. But instead, he held her closer.

Diana asked, "Do you remember what you told me in the laundry room? That I would always be a prisoner in a golden trap? You were wrong. Because you set me free. From the moment I realized that I loved you, I didn't care what I might lose as long as I could keep you. Do you believe me?"

Paul nodded.

"And then, another time, in the little house, you told me—"

"I told you a lot of nonsense. But I had an excuse. I felt as if I were caught in a trap, too. I was fighting against the love that drew me irresistibly to you."

Diana drew back and looked at him severely.

"That's the price you pay when you ignore Private Property and No Swimming signs. It follows you for the rest of your life!"

"And to think I might have gone merrily on my way, instead of heading straight for danger!"

Both fell silent, their faces bathed in the shadowy light of evening. They knew that the time for playing with words and tossing quips back and forth was over. They had tried to adopt the old lighthearted approach but had failed. A month of solitary sadness had taught them the true value of love and their urgent need for each other.

Twilight closed in around their two silhouettes as their lips met.

And then there was silence.

MYSTIQUE BOOKS

Experience the warmth of love... and the threat of danger!

MYSTIQUE BOOKS are a breathless blend of romance and suspense, passion and mystery. Let them take you on journeys to exotic lands—the sunny Caribbean, the enchantment of Paris, the sinister streets of Istanbul.

MYSTIQUE BOOKS

An unforgettable reading experience.
Now... many previously published titles are once again available.
Choose from this great selection!

Don't miss any of these thrilling novels of love and adventure!